CS THOMPSON

WHY NOW?

THE NIGHT THE WOLVES
ESCAPED FROM BAYS MOUNTAIN

A SIXTH NATASHA McMORALES MYSTERY

Published in the U.S. by:
James One Institute
Bristol, TN

Csthompsonbooks.com

ISBN: 978-0-99046-010-7

This is a work of fiction. Names, characters, events and incidents are either the products of the author's imagination or are used in a fictitious manner.

Although the major characters are all fictional and any resemblance to a real person is accidental and unintentional, many of the places and events are real and the people one would find there are real as well.

Cover design by CS Thompson & Cam Collins (www.camelliadigital.com)
Interior design by Gary A. Rosenberg (www.thebookcouple.com)

Contents

Acknowledgments

A special thanks to those who made significant editorial contributions: Anne Southerland, Bob Land, and Sarah Barker.

And for all sorts of advice and support: Barb Thompson, Bonnie McDonald, Cam Collins, Carol and Gary Rosenberg, Craig McDonald, DeeDee Galliher, Dyan Buck, Jenny Hensley, Jill Phelps, and Meredith Harbour.

A special thanks to Jack Southerland, whose original idea got this plotline started.

Also for the twenty-four people who allowed me to "borrow" their real names. Some I described as they are, and others I took creative license with. They all gave their permission. A detailed list of names can be found in the appendix.

NOTE: With the exception of The Saloon in Chattanooga, all locations are real and exist as they are described.

In **Kingsport, TN**: Bagel Exchange, Baker's Jewelry, Bays Mountain, Betty's Stockyard Café, Broad Street, The Carousel Project, Haggle

House, Hibbert-Davis Coffee Shop,JanMar, P & J Antiques, Purple Cow, Suzanne Barrett Justis Gallery, The Meadowview, The Mustard Seed Café, The Nutty Java II, and VIP Seen

In **Bristol, TN**: Blackbird Bakery, Bristol Motor Speedway, Citizens Bank, CityMug, Holston Valley Ruritan Club, Machiavelli's, Manna Bagel, Perkins, Pretty Girl Station, Sessions 27, State Street, The Enchanted Florist and The Grind House

In **Chattanooga, TN:** Alleia's, Aretha Frankenstein's, Big River Brewing Company, Blue Grass Grill, Creative Discovery Museum , Hot Chocolatier, Stone Fort Inn, and Urban Stack Burger Lounge

In **Johnson City, TN**: Earth Fare, Hands On Museum, Rita's, and Tomy Thai

Prologue [Jack Stout]

HI, MY NAME IS JACK STOUT. Well, that isn't actually my name, but it has been my name since the sixth grade. My given name is Alexander Sebastian Stout, and yes, I know what those initials are. I'm named after my father, and he knows what those initials mean, too. When someone refers to him by his initials he just smiles and says, "At your service."

Since my father was already Alexander, I became Sebastian Stout. That is who I was until the third grade, when, on the first day of school, the teacher called roll. "Alexander Stout," she repeated several times. On a whim I decided to tell her I was a Stout, but not the Alexander she was looking for.

"Yes, you are," she told me, "and there is already another Sebastian in this class." Can you imagine the gall? The audacity? I did not know then what those words meant, but I knew the phenomena when I saw it, and I was looking at it then.

I decided to let it pass. I'd let my mother handle whatever the mistake was the next day. As soon as I got home I told my mother that my teacher had told me I wasn't Sebastian Stout. "Well, that's right, Sebastian, you are really Alexander Stout." I don't remember being upset by losing my name because some other poor kid was named Sebastian. I don't even remember being upset that my parents, who had never given me a reason to doubt their trustworthiness, had never given me my given name. My teacher, a virtual stranger on that first day, gave me my given name. But it was not going to stick.

Shortly into my sixth-grade year we moved to Berkeley Heights, New Jersey. My next-door neighbor, Kenny Lynch, became my first and one of my best friends. Kenny was a seventh grader, which meant he went to junior high school, and there was already an Alexander in his class. Kenny gave me the name "Jack." So then, for the second time, I was given a new name by a virtual stranger and all because there was another kid with that name, only this time the other kid was not even in my class. He wasn't even in my school.

Why "Jack?" you might wonder. I don't know. I vaguely recall it was connected to a television show he liked, but that was over fifty years ago, so I don't remember. Nor do I care. So, now, as I said before, I'm Jack. Although Jack is not my given name, it was given to me, and now after nearly half a century I have taken it. If another virtual stranger tries to give me another name, I won't be taking it. Some strangers have even tried to give me a new name as they drove by me in anger. But I don't accept new names anymore, no matter how colorful. And sometimes strangers driving by get my name exactly right, although I'll never understand how they know my name and all my initials.

I am a building inspector in Kingsport, Tennessee. It is a job that allows me to support my family and to get them all through college and out of the house. I suppose I do well enough to afford luxury vacations if I planned it, but planning ahead is Alice's department. My job isn't particularly exciting. Mostly, I deal with two groups of people: those who know what they are doing and those who don't. Contractors generally know what they are doing and are easy to get along with. They understand the rules and will only push on them when they are crunched for time, which is almost always. They ask for flexibility. I explain the flexibility they can have. It is all very amicable. Most contractors want to protect their reputations for the future, so doing things the right way, which may be inconvenient at times is still the best business strategy.

Then there are the contractors who don't know what they are doing. They may know how to build, but they don't know how to run a business as a builder. These folks want to make as much money as they can on every job they do, which always means cutting corners. And cutting corners always means poor construction. Homeowners, and even most developers, only know what cosmetic things to look for in a building. It is the things you cannot see that can cause real friction between bad contractors and building inspectors.

Lucky for us those types of contractors tend to go out of business. Avery Heart was one of those contractors. He and I clashed many times. It was normal procedure for him to "forget" to tar the outside of a foundation before he backfilled it. Then when told it hadn't been inspected yet, his standard reply was, "You were late and it looked like rain."

"Dig it up," I'd say.

Then the game would begin. I'd wait to watch the foundation dug up, and Avery would say, "I'm trying to get the Cat from another job site." This happened three times, and he was always able to outwait me. By the time I could return, the foundation would be uncovered and tarred.

Mr. Avery Heart is no longer in business. He apparently cut too many corners while adding a home office for the wealthiest lawyer in town. We had butted heads over several aspects of that job, but the cut corner that did him in was not one that I had inspected. The lawyer had a collection of valuables. A page from a Wittenberg Bible, a Picasso, several other paintings by people I never heard of, some jewelry, and other collectibles. I'll bet he had a Hank Aaron rookie card. Anyway, his collection was too large for a conventional safe, so he had a contractor build a safe room according to the manufacturer's specifications he had acquired himself. He paid to have it done right and had ensured that it would be done right by making the contractor sign documents of completion saying so. That turned out to be Mr. Heart's undoing after the safe was cleaned out. Someone simply dismantled the exterior paneling and emptied it.

Heart Construction went under after the lawyer's insurance company was done with it. I was called in as a witness to the kinds of practices he had engaged in in the past. If that were not bad enough, his attempt to file bankruptcy brought the scrutiny of the IRS. That's a group that *really* frowns on cutting corners. Avery Heart is still in prison somewhere in New Jersey.

The other group, the one that doesn't know what it's doing, is mostly made up of do-it-yourself homeowners. These folks often feel as if they should be able to do whatever they want to do on their own property. To some extent I agree with that; at least I agree philosophically. On a practical level I want to say, "You should be able to build any kind of firetrap you want as long as you take care of it yourself when it burns and you can make sure it stays clear of your neighbors." I don't say that for fear the homeowner would agree, which is an easy thing to say until the fire starts.

Relating to Kingsport homeowners on a professional basis is why I live in Bristol. The building inspector in Bristol lives in Johnson City, and yes, the Johnson City building inspector lives in Kingsport. It is the building inspector way. Doug Hout, the Kingsport building inspector before me, told me, "Son, you can work where you live but you can't live where you work." Yes, I know, that doesn't entirely make sense, but that was Doug. He was the dullest man I ever met. He never understood why his name was funny. People would say, "Doug Hout canoe," and he'd ask, "Can I what?" The joke that circulated through the last conference I went to was, "What do building inspectors use for birth control?" "Personality." The first time I heard that joke I immediately thought of Doug.

I know the building inspector from Johnson City lives in Kingsport because he called in an anonymous tip. His neighbor was building a deck. It is the kind of project that homeowners think is harmless, but somewhere in America there is a fatal deck collapse every two hours. Actually I have no idea if that is true, but it is the kind of statistical reference old Doug Hout could pull off without being questioned.

When I called on this taxpayer, a kindly old gentleman named Gaylord Crandell, to inform him that he'd need to tear his deck apart and redig the footers, he took a swing at me. He was a bit on the feeble side and he telegraphed his punch so it was a miss, but come on, he took a swing at me. Imagine if I lived down the street from him.

CHAPTER 1

Nathan Calls

"DON'T HANG UP," HE BLURTED WHEN SHE ANSWERED. "I can explain everything."

I doubt that, thought Nattie. She was mad. It had been two weeks since she had heard from Nathan. Two weeks ago she would have said they were on track to get back together. He had been there for her through one of the most challenging cases of her career. He had been there for her even to the point of neglecting his own business. Then, when the case was all over and she found herself back in the hospital, he was by her side through that, too. Then, when she was ready to trust him again, he disappeared. They were supposed to have lunch with Kevin and Knox, but he didn't show. It was a tossup as to what she was angrier about: his disappearance or getting her hopes up before he did it.

He continued, "I know you're upset."

"Upset! Upset doesn't begin to describe what I am." Her voice was crisp and edgy.

"I was trying to protect you from what was happening to me," he pleaded.

It's always about you, isn't it?

"They took the bar, but that's okay," he continued. "I just didn't want you to have to worry about that. And now . . ."

"Wait a minute," she interrupted him. "What do you mean, 'They took the bar'? Who took the bar?"

"The bank did, but it's okay. Really, Nattie, it's okay. I never should have tried to own a bar. You were right. An alcoholic owning a bar," he snorted. "What was I thinking?"

"Banks don't just take businesses, Nathan."

"Banks foreclose on businesses all the time," he said, raising his voice. "Just look around."

"Nathan," she said sternly, "how long have you been in trouble with the bank?" She knew they most likely warned him several times before seizing his assets. She knew it was Citizens Bank that held the note. Citizens was locally owned and operated. They did not want to own a bar, and they didn't want to have to sell it either. They would have worked with him, even to the point of giving business advice. All he had to do was cooperate with them. But she knew him, too. When the going got tough he'd shut down, and if it got worse he'd disappear. This was all too familiar.

He laughed. "I'm not in trouble anymore. The bar is gone, and so are all the headaches that went with it."

"So where have you been for the last two weeks?"

"I told you I was going away for a while," he said defensively.

"No," she said firmly, "you didn't."

"I had to get my head together, you know, retreat . . . regroup . . . plan out my next move."

She knew he had sidestepped her question and lied about having told her. *Why else would you begin with "Don't hang up" and "I can explain"?* "So did you?"

"Did I what?"

"Did you get your head together?"

"I did. Wait until you hear what I've got going on."

"I'm not interested, Nathan."

"Are you serious? I've been through hell here, and now that I'm past it all, the only thing I want to do is share it with you. I just wanted to be in a place where you could be proud of me. I'm always thinking about you. I love you, don't you know that?"

"Look, Nathan, I do believe that you thought about me. I believe that you love me, but when couples who are together go through tough times, they go through them together. You may have wanted me to be proud of you, but what I wanted was to be able to count on you."

"You can," he said urgently. "You can count on me now. Just listen to me, please; give me five minutes and you'll see. I've landed on my feet. Well, I've almost landed on my feet. It's a perfect job for me. For us, really. Let me tell you about it."

"Us? There is no 'us,' Nathan."

"Nattie, I don't blame you. You have every right to feel that way. But we are an 'us,' Nattie, and I will spend the rest of my life proving it to you if I need to."

She stayed quiet.

"You remember that insurance company I used to call on? The one out of Chicago?"

"Federation Fidelity?"

"Yeah, them. Well, they have investigators to look into suspicious claims."

"And they hired you?" asked Nattie without trying to hide her surprise. He was a licensed private investigator at one point, but his license was revoked due to a second DUI. There was almost no chance he would ever be licensed again.

"Not exactly. When they close those cases internally, they open them up to independent contractors."

"So you're not on their payroll."

"No, but I don't want to be either."

Of course, who'd want a regular paycheck and benefits?

"I'm on their independent contractor list," he continued, "and that means I'll have access to their files like an employee, but I'd be working for a percentage of what we recover. The cases will be a little tougher, but the payoffs will be so much better."

"We?"

"Yeah, we. Come on, Nattie, you know we could make a great team. I'll do all the networking to get the cases. And I'll do all the initial work. You don't have to get involved until I get stuck, and even then you don't have to get involved unless you think it's worth your time. For you it's a no-investment, no-risk deal. I'll cover all my expenses, and I'll split all the profit with you for any case you get involved in."

What's the catch? she wondered.

"No risk, no investment," he repeated.

"What do you need me for then?"

"I'm glad you asked. There are two reasons, and the first one is more important. I think we make a great team. You are clearly a better investigator than I am. But I am a better schmoozer than you are. I can get us jobs that you can't get and you can finish jobs I can't finish."

"And the second reason?" she asked.

"I don't need a PI license, but I do have to be affiliated with a licensed agency."

"That means I'll have to bond you, Nathan."

"It means I'll have to be bonded, but I can cover that expense. Like I said, I'll cover all my expenses."

"Okay," she said. "I'll think about it and let you know."

"What's to think about? There's no risk."

"Maybe not financially, but there are other issues for me to consider. Is there a reason to hurry?"

"Sort of," he said. "I'm also going to need you bail me out of jail."

She almost didn't ask. "Why are you in jail, Nathan?"

"DUI."

She turned her phone off, wishing it was the old-fashioned kind of phone, the kind that could be slammed.

9

CHAPTER 2

The O'Briens' Trip

"OH, HE'S NOT GOING TO BE HAPPY," SAID NATTIE'S MOM, Ingrid, as she and Nattie watched Lionel point at the Tri-Cities Airport gift shop. Lionel had gotten their boarding passess while Ingrid and Nattie chatted about the relationship between Nattie's brother, Kevin, and his new love, Knox. It was the kind of conversation Lionel had just as soon miss anyway.

"Why isn't he going to be happy?" asked Nattie.

"He's looking for something to read while he's on the plane, and I told him they don't sell books here."

"So is he going to be angry because they don't sell books or because you told him so?"

Ingrid grinned, "I don't really need to answer that, do I?"

"Are you sure they don't sell books here?" asked Nattie.

"You'd think they would. Lots of people pass the time on planes and in airports with books. But they don't."

"And you've got your Kindle."

"Of course."

Nattie looked out the window toward the airfield and slowly shook her head. "A week in the Caribbean at one of those all-inclusive places.

I'd probably gain twenty pounds. Say, is he going to be comfortable with all the drinking?" Nattie tended to see her stepfather as legalistic in the expression of his faith. And it was true when she had lived with them.

"He'll be fine," said Ingrid. "It's not like it will be a drunken orgy, and besides, he's not as much a reactionary as you think."

"And he won the trip at a convention," noted Nattie.

"And he won the trip," agreed Ingrid. "Are you alright?"

There it is, thought Nattie, *the mother question.* She knew it was coming, and she knew it would come before Lionel returned.

"I'm fine, Mom."

"I know you are," said Ingrid as she slid her arm around Nattie's waist. "You're always fine, but you haven't heard from him in three weeks. I just wish I wasn't leaving the country for a week right now."

Nattie had not shared the phone call she had gotten from Nathan two days earlier. Her Nathan turned out to be a replay of her father, Nathan, Ingrid's first husband. Nathan, the father, was a charming Peter Pan type who could almost always make them laugh until he hit a little girl with his car. That's when he traded his soul for alcohol. That's when Ingrid had packed up her two kids and came home to the Tri-Cities. This Nathan was another Peter Pan who could make her laugh, but whenever life got tough for him he'd hide in a bottle. This Nathan had not killed anyone with his car, yet. As far as she was concerned, it was only a matter of time, and time was what she was no longer willing to invest.

As if Ingrid knew what her daughter was thinking, she pulled Nattie more snuggly against her side, and in a soft voice she said, "Nathan's not your father."

"Oh, but he is," reacted Nattie. "They have the same personality. They have the same vice; my word, Mom, they have the same name. There isn't a psychotherapist in the country who wouldn't tell me I had married my father. I can hear it now: 'You married him so you could save him . . . to make up for not saving your father.'"

"You can think what you want, Nattie," said Ingrid, "but there is still a big difference between them."

"Okay, Mom, I'll bite. What's the difference?"

"Both of them start drinking when they get knocked down, but with your Nathan, he gets back up."

Pulling her head back as far as she could in her mother's embrace, Nattie took a long look at her mother.

They looked intently at each other for a moment. "When your father got knocked down, he just refused to get back up."

"How many times did Dad get back up before he refused to get up?"

"As far as I know, life only knocked him down once. It would have been better for him if he had to face more difficulties earlier. It might have toughened him up for the doozy that knocked him out."

"That really was a doozy," said Nattie.

"It was, but he had a family. Doozy or not, he *had* to get up." Ingrid looked away and flinched her lips, "But he didn't."

It was the first time Nattie had heard her mother talk about her father like this. It was the first time Nattie had thought about that time from her mother's point of view. She realized that she was the same age as her mother when her mother had left her father. This was no time, however, to push the conversation further. Luckily this was the moment Lionel returned.

"Gum, anyone?" Lionel offered.

Nattie shook her head no.

"When we take off," said Ingrid—with Nattie still in the grasp of her left arm, she took hold of Lionel's arm with her right hand—"we have a two-hour layover in Atlanta. We'll get you something to read then."

"Thanks again for bringing us to the airport," Lionel said to Nattie. Then he picked up their carry-on bags and lifted his eyebrows.

Ingrid smiled at Nattie, explaining, "That's my cue that it's time to go."

After a hug from Ingrid, Nattie held her arms out to hug Lionel. He had to bend over to receive his hug. She found it amusing that her kiss on his cheek made him blush slightly.

Nattie watched them take their place at the back of the slow-moving line through security until her phone vibrated in her hand. It was a text from Hiram Moreland, her old mentor and Nathan's uncle. The text read, "Call me ASAP. Nathan in hospital."

CHAPTER 3

St. Lucia [Jack]

I'VE BEEN MARRIED TO ALICE FOR FORTY YEARS. It has been a great forty years. We have four great kids and six grandkids to show for it. The grandkids are great, too, but we aren't great grandparents, if you know what I mean. You would not accuse us of being adventurous. Alice would tell you that if it costs money or rocks the boat, then I'm not going to want to do it. I suppose she's right. Mostly right anyway. That's why I booked an excursion to a Sandals resort in St. Lucia. I didn't blink twice at the cost when the lady at AAA showed it to me. I wanted it to be expensive. I wanted to show Alice she was worth it to me. I didn't have second thoughts either.

At least I didn't have second thoughts right away. My first *Uh-oh, what have I done* moment came on the airplane when we were stowing our carry-ons. Alice's rotator cuff tear made it impossible for her to lift her bag up. My camera bag was in my left hand, and a coffee and my carry-on were in my right. She took my coffee, and I attempted to stow her carry-on overhead without putting mine down in the aisle. Of course the plane was full and everyone was already seated, so I, with an unwanted audience, did what I always do in awkward moments. I tried to hurry up and get it over with as fast as possible. And I almost pulled it off. I got both bags lifted high enough. I was thankful for that. But as soon as it was over my head, Alice's bag, which I held by a flexible handle, began to circle away from its target. With my other hand full, there was nothing I could do but watch it drift in slow motion over the head of another passenger. He was wearing a fedora hat. I had a great view of his eyes. They got bigger and bigger.

Lucky for the fedora hat, the man behind him stood up and took control of Alice's bag. It was a very thoughtful and gracious thing to do. I was thankful and told him so as I lifted my bag to stow next to Alice's. That's when he treated me like an old man. He took my bag, a bag I was handling fine, and "helped" me.

Had anyone been watching? What am I saying? Everyone on that plane was watching, and they saw me shake his hand and tell him thanks. What I hope they could not do was read my mind. In my head I told this youngster that a year ago I would have kicked his butt all over the tennis court.

Age and doing it wrong a whole bunch of times have taught me not to say things like that out loud. But age has had no effect on the snarky comments in my head. As I sat down, I was glad that I at least looked grateful. And it was true I was really that grateful. I was just something else, too. I was embarrassed.

Then another realization hit me. I remembered the thought I had. To the best of my knowledge this was the first time I had ever uttered an imaginary threat with the words, *"A year ago I would have kicked your butt."* A year ago I would have thought, *I could kick your butt,* and now it was, *A year ago I could have kicked your butt.* So age has had an effect on me. There was no denying it. I was now an old fart. And if I'm just figuring that out, then Alice has known it for a while. So my first "second thought" returned with this thought: *I hope Alice isn't having second thoughts.*

CHAPTER 4

The Pavilion

HIRAM LOOKED UP AS NATTIE PULLED IN TO THE PARKING PLACE next to him. They had agreed to meet in the parking lot adjacent to the Pavilion, the psychiatric hospital. Nattie had told Hiram that she wanted no part of Nathan's latest trip through rehab. "It's not a rehab unit," Hiram had told her. "It's a psychiatric unit."

She wasn't sure why the kind of unit it was mattered, but it seemed to matter to Hiram, so she agreed to meet him.

"Thanks for coming," Hiram said as he lumbered out of the car.

She had to be deliberate about not saying, "You're welcome" or "no problem." "Tell me why I'm here, Hi."

"I'm not sure. They just told me they wanted two family members to talk to the doc before they'd discharge him."

"I'm not family anymore," said Nattie.

Glancing in the direction of the Pavilion he said, "That's just a technicality."

You can't look at me and say that, can you? thought Nattie.

"It sounded serious," he continued. Looking back at Nattie he added, "We're all the family he has."

"What sounded serious?" she asked. "Did they tell you what's going on with him?"

"It sounded like he has two personalities."

Nattie took her turn stalling for time by looking at the Pavilion. "Bipolar," she blurted out. "Did they say he has bipolar disorder?"

"That's it," said Hiram, pointing at her.

* * *

"We're Nathan Moreland's family. We have an appointment with Doctor Pepper," Hiram said through the intercom.

Doctor Pepper, repeated Nattie to herself.

"That's Doctor Peppa," said the voice through the intercom. "Come on in."

The door made a robot pig noise and popped open.

As they entered, they were approached by a middle-aged man in a three-piece suit. "I'm Gregory Peppa, Nathan's psychiatrist. This is great timing. I was just standing at the nurses' station when she buzzed you in."

Doctor Peppa was certainly friendly enough, but his handshake was so weak it felt slimy to her. He led them to a conference room. After they were seated, he, still standing, asked, "Did the nurse tell you anything about what Nathan is dealing with?"

"She told us he had bipolar," answered Hiram. "What does that mean?"

"The term means two poles," explained the doctor. "One pole is a high that sometimes looks very creative and energetic, and sometimes it can look wild and out of control. In Nathan's case the highs make resisting alcohol very difficult if not almost impossible. Then there are the lows. They look like depression. Now, I don't have much time right now. I've got a consult in a few minutes, but before he is discharged we'll make an appointment for him with a therapist for ongoing outpatient treatment and family therapy. I'm sure the therapist

17

will be able to spend much more time with you and answer any of your questions."

"Well, no offense, Doc," began Hiram, "but if this other doc is going to be the one to answer our questions, then why were we called in?"

Doctor Peppa smiled at Hiram.

You're been around this block more than once, thought Nattie, watching the doctor handle Hiram.

"I asked you here so that I could ask you a question, and as simple as it might seem it is a critical element in Nathan's treatment."

"What do you want to know?" asked Nattie.

The psychiatrist held up a finger. "Let me explain one more thing and then I'll ask you my question. Nathan came here directly from a DUI lockup; there was no sign of other drug use, but I wouldn't expect that now anyway. His legal issues were resolved because of a malfunction with the breathalyzer apparatus. I'd say he dodged a bullet there because he was undoubtedly guilty. They brought him here because he wasn't sleeping. By the way, periods of little or no sleep is one of the classic symptoms of bipolar disorder. His speech pattern was rapid, his psychomotor movements were agitated, and he was going on and on about some grandiose scheme to get rich finding stolen art treasures. Now, we're going to let you visit with him in a minute and you won't see all the symptoms that I just described. That is because we have him on several medicines to help him sleep and to stabilize his mood. Now, it is critical that he comply with this medicine. Does that make sense to you?"

Nattie and Hiram both nodded in the affirmative.

"Good. Then here is my question. Will one of you commit to calling him every morning and making sure he takes his meds? And will the other call him every evening and do the same?"

Hiram looked at Nattie and shrugged, "I'll take the morning."

"I'll take the evening then," Nattie said, without a thought to the commitment.

"Good," said Dr. Peppa. "I have to run, but if you just wait here, I'll tell them to send Nathan in so that you can talk to him."

Nathan must have been waiting at the door because he came in as soon as the doctor left. "Thanks for coming, guys," he said.

Nattie noticed that his speech was a little faster than normal, but she wasn't entirely sure that it only seemed that way because of what Dr. Peppa had just told them.

"I knew you were mad," Nathan told her as he hugged her tightly, "but I knew you'd come anyway." He let her go and stepped back. "Did they tell you that the DUI case was dropped?"

"Should it have been dropped?" Nattie asked.

He smiled like a five-year-old who had just been caught. "Legally speaking, no. I was guilty." He shrugged, "But ethically speaking, yes, it should have been dropped. Doctor Peppa just told you my drinking problems are related to my diagnosis, didn't he? And how about his name? Huh? I'll bet Kevin would have a field day with it."

"What about that bipolar thing, Nathan? Do you understand what it means?" asked Hiram.

Nathan looked at Hiram and lit up. "Hi," he exclaimed, "thanks for coming."

Hiram stood up and cupped his hand around the back of Nathan's neck. "Are you okay?"

"Actually, I feel great. If they find a counselor for me I might get to go home tomorrow. What's the name of that counselor you know, Nattie?"

"Charlotte Stevens."

"Do you think she'd be good? Do you have her phone number? Do you know what she charges?"

"Slow down," said Hiram. "I'm sure the people here can find her information for you. We have some questions of our own for you. Don't we, Nattie?"

"Yes," she said.

Nathan sat down at the end of the table and folded his hands. "Ask away."

Hiram looked at Nattie and nodded.

"Do you think this diagnosis is right?" she asked.

"Why wouldn't I?"

"Because," Hiram said, "it will probably mean making some changes in your life."

"Yes," agreed Nattie. "We know there's going to be medication you'll have to take. We know that because we just agreed to make sure you take it."

"Thank you for that," Nathan said again.

"I think she wants to know if you're going to cooperate with taking your medicine," added Hiram. "And I want to know if you're going to quit drinking."

Leaning over his still folded hands Nathan said, "I promise. I really mean it. I promise. I know I have made more than my share of mistakes. And I'm pretty sure that Nattie was about to write me off."

Both men looked at Nattie.

"True," she said.

"But you have to believe that I would be excited to have an explanation that gives me something to fix. If you were me you'd be excited to finally understand something that had haunted you for forever."

"Nathan," Nattie said in as serious a tone as she could muster. When she had his full attention she said, "You were right: I was ready to write you off. First when you called me up after disappearing for several weeks, I was tempted to hang up right away, but then you started talking about your new opportunity to investigate insurance fraud cases and I got sucked in again. I was even considering it when you told me that you needed my agency to make it work."

"It will work," he blurted. "You'll see."

Nattie glared at him until he stopped talking. "Do you really think this is a good time to interrupt me?"

"Sorry," he said, scrunching down like a little boy.

"Like I said, I was considering it, but when you told me about that latest DUI, that was it for me. I was done." She held her finger out to ensure that he not speak. "I want you to understand that when I say I was done, I mean I was *done*. If you had called again, I was not going to answer. If you had written, I would not have read it. Do you understand that?"

He nodded. "I don't blame you."

"Frankly, Nathan, I don't care if you blame me or not. All I care about right now is that you understand that this is it. The only, and I mean only, reason I am here is that this explanation is different from any of the excuses I have already heard. So I'm here and I'll help you any way I can as long as you don't drink and as long as you follow through with whatever the doctors tell you to do. If you fail in either of those ways, then I am done."

"I won't let you down," he said. "And for the record, I'm going to make good on the insurance gig. I'll turn over a forty-thousand-dollar claim within the first two days after I get out of here. And I can do that without your agency being involved at all."

"I'm not worried about that right now," Nattie told him.

"Yeah, Nathan," said Hiram, "and maybe you shouldn't worry about that now either. Maybe you should just concentrate on figuring out what to do with this new information."

"You don't believe me, do you?" said Nathan as he tapped his finger on the table.

Nattie and Hiram looked at each other, each hoping the other would respond.

"We don't know what to think about that, Nathan," confessed Nattie. "The doctor told us that grandiose ideas were symptoms of your diagnosis. We just want you to get better."

"That's fine," he said, bobbing his head slightly as he spoke, "but if I just happen to recover four hundred thousand dollars in diamonds, would you let me use your agency as an umbrella? I'll still cover all my own expenses and cut you in on half."

Nattie and Hiram looked at each other again. Hiram gave her a "Why not?" lift of his eyebrows.

"I'll agree to that on the condition that we get the okay for it from your counselor."

"That's fine."

"And I think 10 percent is fine for an agency cut," suggested Nattie.

"Accepted," Nathan said as he extended his hand to shake.

As they shook on it, Nathan lowered his voice to a whisper. "In another week we'll be going after a million dollars in stolen artwork."

CHAPTER 5

Second Uh-Oh [Jack]

THE SECOND *UH-OH, WHAT HAVE I GOTTEN INTO?* **MOMENT** came later the first night. We arrived at the Sandals a little after four o'clock. We checked in, which meant exchanging my credit card number for a little cardboard card that I presume lessens the how-much-am-I-spending awareness. Now that I think of it, this must be what happens to politicians; they get issued a little cardboard card when they get sworn in and lose their 'how-much-am-I spending' awareness. Anyway, this ploy may work on their normal guests and it surely works on politicians, but I am no normal guest and I am no politician. If I were a superhero, I'd be Captain Cheap. I'd have my own comic, and in the first episode I'd fly into Washington and save the U.S. economy by taking away all those little cardboard cards. Then as I fly home, all the people would cheer by making baby chick noises. *Cheep-cheep.*

While I was busy filling out the Sandals paperwork, Alice made reservations for us at the five-star Italian restaurant, The Toscanini. This was the restaurant she was most excited about. It had the lead on the other eateries for multiple evenings. Alice, ever the organizer, had a plan for every evening meal during our first four nights, after which we would decide which places we would bless with our patronage for additional meals.

As I said, Alice is organized. She is as organized as I am not. She knew the Sandals literature inside and out before we got on the plane, before we packed, and before we shopped in order to pack. She knew that the five-star eateries, of which there were two, had a dress code: island formal. Men were required to wear long pants and shirts with sleeves and a collar. They did not require dress shirts and dress pants; it was a Caribbean island after all.

So, to please Alice and to prove to her that I am not Captain Cheap (*cheep cheep*) when it comes to her, I went shopping for new island clothes. My timing could not have been better because Old Navy was offering a 40 percent discount if you signed up for one of their credit cards (*cheep cheep*). I bought two collared shirts, a pair of khaki pants, a swimsuit, and some sandals. I was ready to go.

Once we were settled in our room, which meant marveling at the size of the complimentary shampoo bottle and figuring out how the television worked. Alice emerged from the bathroom with a large green bottle. "Look," she said, "they've stocked the bathroom with aloe."

"Nice," I said, "and they have ESPN." She was not impressed.

She was not impressed with my new pants either. "They're wrinkled," she informed me, "and they have no crease."

"I'll fix it," I promised. And I did. She volunteered to take care of it herself as I set up the iron and ironing board. She watched as I ironed out the wrinkles and put a beautiful crease down my Old Navy khakis. I did not iron up around the pockets as no one would tuck an island shirt in. The crease would not last the evening, but it only needed to get us seated.

When the time came we took our dressed-up selves and made our way to the restaurant. I was styling in my new duds, which would never match how beautiful Alice looked, but that was never the goal. (The goal was to at least avoid comments like, "Is this your daughter?" and looks that said, "That guy must be rich.")

We arrived at the Toscanini fifteen minutes early. Alice even apologized to the hostess, "We're fifteen minutes early." The hostess flashed an enormous toothy smile and uttered the words we would hear all week, "No problem." Then to me she said, "That will give you time to go get shoes."

Alice looked at me like she had been told she was on fire. I looked down at the only shoes I had brought: sandals. I wanted to say, 'How about that crease?' but I didn't. Alice, in more of a plead than an argument, said, "He didn't bring closed-toed shoes. Your literature didn't say to do that."

"No problem," the hostess smiled. "Colored socks will work."

Of course, I thought, *I didn't bring shoes, but I was sure to pack an assortment of different-colored socks to go with my sandals.* What I said was, "Can I buy socks at the shop in the lobby?"

"No problem."

Well, there was a problem. When we got to the shop and asked if they sold socks, the answer was not "No problem." It was just no. I didn't have to look at Alice to picture the look of disappointment on her face. Lucky for me, just outside the Sandals clothes shop were two pool tables where two couples were playing pool. Putting away my don't-make-waves life strategy, I approached the gentleman who looked to be my age. "I'll give you twenty dollars for a used pair of socks." "My only pair," he answered lifting his pant leg so I could see. *Nice crease*, I thought. "Good luck," he smiled. "Thanks."

The younger man, probably on his honeymoon, looked at me like I was either nuts or on a scavenger hunt. "They won't let me in the restaurant," I explained. "It's the one my wife has her heart set on." Ten minutes later he returned with a new pair of black socks. I thanked him profusely, realizing that it was an act of charity rather than finance. I doubt that any guest at a Sandals resort—any guest besides me, that is—is hard up for a twenty-dollar bill.

CHAPTER 6

Getting Comfortable [Jack]

I'M AN EARLY RISER. Even on vacation I'm up between 5:30 and 6 a.m. Alice considers herself an early riser, too. She'll get up between seven and seven-thirty. At home I would use the time alone to make coffee, read, and reconfirm my decision to begin the day with a forty-five-minute walk . . . tomorrow. In St. Lucia I would go park myself at a little table in front of Josephine's. It faced the pool and, beyond that, the ocean. Peaceful. The breeze was always gentle and always carried floral smells, which I love, and which on occasion calls my manhood to question.

I'd have my book open, but mostly I'd watch the staff at work prepping for the day. There was no hurry in any of them. I sure wish I knew how to do that. I'm either on or off. If any of the pool guys caught me watching them, they'd smile and wave at me. Little did they know how much I wanted their jobs. They may have even thought they would want mine. But I knew better.

The one thing I'd change about the view if I could would be the decor around the pool. There was a three-story structure covering the poolside sunken bar touting the large Sandals sign. I can't blame them from wanting to make sure we never forgot where we were, but it blocked some of my view of the ocean. But the decor I really didn't understand was all the Romanesque statues scattered around the pool. Here's a place catering to romantic couples with all the rich food and alcohol they could want, and they decided to make it look like Pompeii. Has anyone heard of Vesuvius?

As for my own decline into self-indulgence, I went willingly. Josephine's opens at six for coffee and continental breakfast and, as I have already said, I'm usually already there pretending to read. Tamika, the server, memorized my routine after the first day. A three-cup pot of coffee at six followed by another pot of decaf at six forty-five. What will become of me if I get used to this kind of service? A picture of Jabba the Hutt floated through my mind.

Alice would be ready to swim laps, or in my case, lap, by seven-thirty. By eight-thirty the breakfast buffet at the Bayside would open, and I'd have to serve myself. Maybe that was a good thing. Something has to keep me humble and my feet anchored to the earth. I realized that there are places on the earth where people have to make their own breakfast. Surely I could fill my own plate.

During breakfast we would decide what we would do for the day. We'd been snorkeling the first two days. Yesterday after breakfast we lounged by the pool. The sunken pool bar opened at ten, but I didn't want to have to get up and go over there for a drink. I had decided to try every blended drink listed on their sign, but I wasn't motivated enough to actually get it myself. I was comforted by the fact that I was laying on my stomach as I read *Once upon a Midlife Crisis* (fitting, don't you think?). Jabba the Hutt couldn't lay on his stomach. Then a bar-maid came to where I lounged and asked if I wanted a drink. "I'll have whatever the first blended drink is," I said. She came back a few minutes later with a Banana Surprise. She watched as I tasted it. 'Good?' she asked. 'Good,' I said. She watched me place the drink on the deck next to my lounge. "Anything else?" she asked. I actually thought about asking for a two-foot straw so that I wouldn't have to reach down to get a drink. Look out, Jabba. Here I come.

CHAPTER 7

Knox

NATTIE WALKED THROUGH HER OFFICE DOOR with her head still swimming from her visit to the psychiatric ward. She had committed to helping Nathan, and breaking a commitment was not a question for her. The question that she vacillated on as she drove across town was whether she was the biggest fool in North America. Getting involved with him again meant trusting his sobriety, which was a big enough risk by itself. *Maybe there's a medicine that will take care of that, but is there one that will take care of pie-in-the-sky fantasies? No, he's feeling good now because they have him drugged up and he's thinking he's going to make a quarter of a million dollars chasing art thieves, but when that goes belly up, he's going to want to run away again.*

At least Kevin, the absolute king of wacky ideas, had the good sense to not bother following through with his pipe dreams.

"Is it that bad?"

The question startled Nattie. She had thought she would be alone because the door was locked and Kevin's car was not in front. "Knox," she said, "what are you doing here?"

"Kevin asked me to answer the phone. Is that okay?"

"Yes, Knox, it's fine. I was just startled is all."

"So," said Knox.

The statement confused Nattie, "I'm sorry?"

"When you first came in I asked you if it was so bad. So—is it?"

"Is what so bad?"

"Is whatever you were worrying over so bad?"

Nattie studied Knox's face before deciding, "I'm glad you're here. I need someone to talk to."

The request seemed to have the effect of improving Knox's posture. As her head went up, her shoulders went back and her smile broadened. She pointed at the waiting room couch in front of them.

"I know you'd be talking to your mom if she wasn't in the Caribbean, but any time I can help you, I will."

Nattie sat down first. As she watched Knox settle in to the seat next to her, she realized how much she missed having a confidante. She still thought of Miranda as the best friend she had ever had. She still smarted from Miranda's death. And then there was Debbie, whose pig of a husband thought their friendship was taking too much time away from their kids.

The thought of Knox as someone to confide in had not yet occurred to Nattie. Knox was first a client, and then she became Kevin's significant other, a relationship that was both surprising and perfect. Knox tended to be oblivious to the world around her and her comments tended to reflect that disconnect, except for the occasional moment of insightfulness. It was a description that fit Kevin as well.

"Thanks, Knox, I appreciate it."

"No, thank you," returned Knox. "Most people don't think of me when they need advice."

Oh great, thought Nattie, *she thinks I want advice.*

"Kevin said you were at the hospital visiting Nathan. Is that what's bothering you?"

"Yes. Tell me, how much has Kevin already told you about Nathan and me?"

29

Knox flinched backward slightly at the question.

"It's okay, Knox. I know you guys talk. I'm sure when Nathan stood us up for lunch several weeks ago that Kevin filled you in on some background. I just wanted to know how much I need to tell you."

Knox's shoulders relaxed. "I know you were married. I know that you still love each other. And I know that you divorced him because of his drinking and that he has been trying to win you back. Is that right?"

The summation Knox gave was brief, but it covered all the necessary points. The fact that it could be covered so simply both surprised and saddened Nattie.

"You've got the basic picture, but it wasn't his drinking that caused the divorce. It was his refusal to face it. Basically it was his irresponsibility. I just couldn't count on him."

"He comes off as pretty responsible when you meet him, but I know some people can appear one way and be another."

"True," said Nattie.

"I'm sure that most people would say Kevin is irresponsible, but if you are counting on him, he won't let you down."

"That's true," agreed Nattie. "And that's been the problem between Nathan and me. He would disappear when I needed him the most."

Knox's eyebrows flexed.

"What is it?" asked Nattie.

"Nothing. I mean it's just hard to picture you needing anyone. You're the most self-sufficient person I ever met. Did he know you needed him."

"How could he not know?" reacted Nattie. "We were married. He's an adult. He shouldn't need to be told I needed him."

"Sorry, I didn't mean to upset you. I've just noticed that Nathan works really hard at being a grown-up. It kinda sticks out because

Kevin doesn't work at that at all. It makes me wonder why he is trying so hard."

"Me, too. But whatever it is that's going on inside his head is his to face. Facing difficulties, though, has never been his strength."

"So what is he facing now? Or should I ask, what is he supposed to be facing now?"

"Bipolar disorder," answered Nattie. "That's the diagnosis they gave him at the hospital."

"That's good, isn't it?"

"Why would that be good?"

"If he's got it, then it's good that he knows he's got it," said Knox tentatively. "You want him to face it, right?"

Nattie nodded.

"Well, I don't see how he could face it if he didn't know he had it." When Knox finished speaking, she looked long and hard at Nattie. "Did I say something wrong?"

"No, why?"

"You were looking at me like I was saying something wrong."

"No, sorry. I was just thinking about what you were saying. You're right. I should be looking at this as a positive thing." She rubbed the back of her neck and took a deep breath before continuing. "But that's the problem. The fact that there's something new to explain things makes me want to hope on him, and so far, hoping on him has never worked out for me."

"Do you have to decide right now if you trust him?"

"No, I don't. I committed to helping him with his medications and to come to his family counseling, but that's all so far."

"Do you want it to be more?"

"Yes."

"But you don't trust it to be more?"

"No, I don't."

"Is there any pressure on you to decide that now?"

"Just my own."

Knox lifted her shoulders. "Why don't you just ride out the diagnosis for a while and see how that goes?"

"That's good advice." She reached out and held Knox's hand. "You know, I didn't really want advice. I just wanted you to listen, but I'm glad it went this way."

Knox blushed as she gently squeezed Nattie's hand.

"Do you want to hear something funny?" asked Nattie.

"Sure."

"Nathan's psychiatrist is Doctor Peppa."

"Doctor Pepper," repeated Knox. "Like the soda?"

"Peppa, not Pepper, but close enough."

Knox grinned. "Kevin is going to have fun with that one."

CHAPTER 8

Charlotte Stevens

[The next day.]

NATTIE KNEW EXACTLY WHERE CHARLOTTE STEVENS'S office was. She had never met the woman herself, but she had recommended her based on what Callie Trainor had said about her. Callie was a suspect in a previous case, and Nattie had followed her to Charlotte Stevens's office several times. Their appointment was for four o'clock. They were told to come fifteen minutes early to fill out the paperwork. A friendly woman greeted her as she entered the waiting room. "Hi, I'm Dyan. Are you here to see Dr. Stevens?"

"I'm supposed to meet Nathan Moreland here," she said, "but I don't think he's here."

Dyan handed her a clipboard. "You can go ahead with the paperwork, if you want."

Nattie looked at her watch. It was three-fifty. Nathan was nowhere in sight.

As Nattie toyed with the idea of leaving, the door at the back of the waiting room opened, and in walked Charlotte Stevens. She was in her fifties, just under six feet tall, freckles, and straight auburn hair that hung down to her waist. She accented the plain floral dress she wore with a macramé necklace. "I'm Charlotte Stevens," she said, her eyes fully focused on Nattie. "Are you here to see me?"

"I'm Nattie Moreland," she explained. "I'm supposed to be here with Nathan Moreland for family counseling, but he's not here yet." She held out the untouched paperwork. "I wasn't sure what to do with this."

"Nathan will need to be the one to fill out the paperwork. He's really the client. You're here in a support role, so none of that is necessary for you." Charlotte then extended her hand toward the open door. "Nathan called and said he was running late but that he is on the way. He said he's coming back through Sam's Gap and got behind a jack-knifed truck. He gave me permission to talk to you, so we might as well get to know each other."

Charlotte's therapy room was the way Nattie had pictured a therapy room. It was well lit with natural light coming through windows that lined two of the four walls. In the middle of the room was a coffee table and on it the proverbial box of tissues. Four cushy chairs surrounded the coffee table. On one of the chairs was a clipboard and pen. Finishing off the room were several plants and pieces of art.

Charlotte sat in the chair that held the clipboard. Nattie took the chair across from her.

"I met with Nathan this morning just after he was discharged. He seems to have accepted Doctor Peppa's diagnosis. How about you?"

"I don't know," said Nattie. "It could be an answer." She wanted to stop talking, but Charlotte just watched her like she knew she had more to say. "It could be an excuse, too."

"It will be up to him which one it is."

"Do you think he's bipolar?"

"I prefer to say he has bipolar disorder rather than he is bipolar. If he does have it—and I can't verify that one way or the other at this point—but if he does have it, then it will explain some aspects of his life, but not his whole being."

Hippie, thought Nattie. "So you're not sure about that diagnosis yet."

"No, I'm not. But then again I don't much care about his diagnosis just yet." She studied Nattie's reaction. "Right now I'm really concerned about what he wants. You see, I'm not going to be of much use to him unless he wants something."

"You want to know if he's motivated," interpreted Nattie.

"Yes. In my experience everyone wants to be different but only a few want to change. If he doesn't want to change anything, then it doesn't much matter what his diagnosis is. Do you think he wants to change?"

"I hope so," said Nattie.

"He told me that you'd be skeptical."

"I don't mean to be," said Nattie, a little embarrassed by the comment.

"Don't give it a second thought," assured Charlotte. "It sounds to me like he's given you every reason to be skeptical. You are skeptical, aren't you?"

"I am."

"Do you want to tell me about it?"

"I think he's an alcoholic, but I don't think he's really admitted that to himself. I know I have my own baggage about his drinking. My father was—I mean, is—an alcoholic. He and my mother split up when I was in junior high. Nathan and he are a lot alike. They're both charming salesmen types who can talk their way into opportunities without considering what it takes to work them through. And they both act like they can just talk their way out of trouble."

"What's your father's name?" asked Charlotte as she wrote on her clipboard.

When Nattie answered "Nathan," Charlotte lifted her eyes to see Nattie's reaction.

How did you know to ask that? wondered Nattie.

As if she had heard Nattie's thought, Charlotte said, "That question was just a lucky guess. I don't want you to think I have some magical mind-reading powers."

Too late for that, thought Nattie.

"Please go on," Charlotte told her.

"Aside from all their similarities, I don't believe that I'm projecting my issues with my father on to my husband."

"Your husband," repeated Charlotte.

Nattie paused, "Did I say 'my husband'?"

Charlotte nodded yes.

"What does that mean?"

"What does it mean to you?" asked Charlotte.

"I don't think it means I still think of Nathan as my husband."

"Okay," said Charlotte.

"You don't believe me, do you?" asked Nattie.

Charlotte smiled. "I believe that you know you and he are divorced, but I don't believe that you are 100 percent done thinking of him as family."

"I believe I am," said Nattie.

"And yet," observed Charlotte, "here you are in his family counseling session."

Squinting, Nattie studied the therapist for a moment and then slowly asked, "Am I being analyzed?"

"Does it seem that way?"

"As a matter of fact, it does. Especially when you answer questions with questions."

Charlotte clinched her teeth together and placed the fingertips of her right hand on her sternum. "Did I do that? I'm sorry about that. I suppose I need to be more aware of myself, don't I?" She put her hand down and took a deliberate breath. "Let me answer your question. I am not analyzing in the manner Freud would. In fact, that isn't my style as a general rule. But I was assessing your commitment to the recovery of Mr. Moreland, and I really am sorry if that felt intrusive to you."

"I understand," said Nattie. "I just wasn't sure where we were headed with all that stuff about whether or not I still feel like he's my husband."

"I wasn't trying to head us anywhere in particular. It was my intention to establish a working relationship with you. I was just responding to what you were saying with interest and curiosity. The truth is that I was really expecting this session to include Mr. Moreland."

"Me, too," said Nattie as she took out her phone and began dialing.

As soon as Nattie lifted her phone to her ear she heard loud guitar music come from the other side of the door. She looked at Charlotte, who shrugged and shook her head no.

"There's no way my office manager, Dyan, would let anyone be there right now," stated Charlotte firmly.

Standing and gesturing for silence with her finger against her lips, Nattie went over and stood next to the door. She turned the handle slowly, and then with a sudden jerk she threw the door open. Without looking to see who was there she said, "Hello, Nathan."

CHAPTER 9

Last Night at Sandals [Jack]

ALICE WANTED OUR LAST NIGHT AT THE RESORT TO BE SPECIAL, so she put off deciding which of the restaurants to go to. We had loved Barefoot by the Bay the most, but we had only been to Toscanini once, so Toscanini it was. Alice had her eye on the lamb, and I loved the carbonara I had the first night, so I was happy. Besides, I was already prepared with the required colored socks for my sandals. That begs the question: Why aren't sandals good enough for Sandals?

Toscanini's not only required socks; they required reservations as well. They probably would have accommodated us without reservations if they had not been completely booked. They were apologetic, and we were gracious. As we turned to go, the older gentleman standing behind us said, "Please wait." Apparently he had heard our whole conversation, so he asked the hostess if his was a table for two or a table for four. "We can seat you at either," she told him. "Make it a table for four," he said. As soon as he said this, his wife smiled at Alice and said, "Join us."

That is the story of how we met Lionel and Ingrid O'Brien. Actually, it was the second time we had met, but I was not to discover that until we had been seated for a while. You see, I was a bit distracted because of a text message I had received just before we came down to dinner. Our daughter, Juney (short for Juniper), was taking care of our home and our dog, Mariah. She was there when a court summons was delivered. "Just pretend you didn't get it," advised Alice. "There's nothing you can do about it 'til you get home anyway." As it turned out, it was a stroke of good fortune that she let us know.

"I see you got your socks," said Lionel with a grin.

That's when I looked closer. He was the older gentleman whom I had first approached with my twenty-dollar offer. He and Ingrid watched me closely as recognition came to me. We all had a good laugh. I was sorry now that I had thought of him as the "older gentleman." I'm fifty-five, and I'll bet Lionel is no more than ten or so years my senior. He simply looks a hundred years more distinguished than I. I decided that the phrase "older gentleman" is code for a man who has aged gracefully. "Old fart" is code for a man who did not. As I said before, I am an old fart. I wasn't sure what "old cuss" was code for, but I immediately thought of Doug Hout.

"If I had had a second pair, I'd have given them to you," said Lionel. Then to Alice he added, "I almost gave him this pair when he told us you would be brokenhearted if you could not get in."

"And if you had given him that pair, we wouldn't be here tonight," observed Alice.

"Where are you guys from?" asked Ingrid.

"Tennessee," Alice informed her. We always answer that way. We assume that Tennessee is specific enough when you are on the other side of the world, but we are always surprised when we are far from home and people recognize Bristol. "NASCAR," they usually say.

"Where in Tennessee?" questioned Ingrid. "We're from Johnson City."

"Bristol," said Alice, pointing at herself.

I was surprised that no one said, "It's a small world," but Ingrid did turn to Lionel and ask, "Didn't you take flying lessons with a man from Bristol?"

"John Vann," stated Lionel. "He's the chairman of the United Way. Do you know him?"

Now Bristol, Tennessee, is no teeny little podunk town. We are the Birthplace of Country Music. We have two major NASCAR events and the Rhythm & Roots music festival every year. To assume that everyone in Bristol knows everyone else in Bristol is to relegate us to some sort of inferior standing. What was so metropolitan about Johnson City, anyway? They have ETSU and the Mall.

"Yes," I told him. "We know John very well. He and his wife, Karen, were in a Bible study with us."

"What did you study?" asked Lionel. He seemed pleased that we were in a Bible study. The question was no surprise considering that we both lived in the buckle of the Bible belt.

"We did a read-through-the-Bible-in-a-year program with four other couples," explained Alice, "and then we did a study of David together. It was great fellowship, but it came to an end when one of the couples moved."

"That's too bad," said a serious Lionel. Then, taking Ingrid's hand, he said, "We felt like being part of a small group like that really helped us grow. We had a small group we belonged to, but we were the youngsters and everyone else retired and moved away. We really miss it."

"I know what you mean," said Alice. "We really miss our group, too. I think it's easy for women to get intimacy at church, but the men in our group really got close too in our group."

"And John Vann was part of that," confirmed Lionel.

"He was," I told them just before Alice told me to tell the pancake story. "The pancake story: All the men in our growth group went away for a weekend together. We stayed in a cabin up near Grandfather Mountain. Each of us took a turn cooking. Breakfast the last day was

John's turn. He got up early Sunday morning and made us his 'famous' oatmeal pancakes. There was no spatula to flip, with so he used the other kind of spatula, the kind you use to get the last of the mayonnaise from the bottom of the jar."

"The soft, rubbery kind?" asked Ingrid.

"Yes," I said, "the kind of soft rubber that melts. By the time he made a full platter of those pancakes, all that was left of that spatula was the wooden stick."

CHAPTER 10

Nathan's Announcement

NORMALLY WHEN NATTIE CAUGHT NATHAN doing something he shouldn't, he'd flash a little-boy, aren't-I-cute-anyway smile at her, but this smile was different. It was more of a smirk. *Is that the bipolar?* wondered Nattie. *He's got nothing to smirk about.*

As he stepped past her into the room, he tipped his head to the side and leaned toward her left cheek. When Nattie pulled back, his proud smirk morphed into a grin.

I wonder if you'd look different if we weren't in your doc's office?

"Hi, doc," he said as he turned from Nattie.

"Mr. Moreland," Charlotte said as she gestured to a chair.

"How are you two getting along? Talking about me, I suppose."

After glancing at her watch, Charlotte said, "You are half an hour late, Mr. Moreland. Is that really how you want to begin?"

Nattie sat back down. She studied the therapist while the therapist studied Nathan. It was Nattie's turn to smirk as she thought, *She's gonna be good for you.* "Mr. Moreland."

"I'm sorry I'm late," he said to Charlotte first, then again to Nattie.

"Thank you," said Charlotte. "Would you like to add anything to that?"

He stood up quickly. "Actually I would." His eyes darted quickly back and forth between the two women. "I can't wait to tell you both why I'm late." Then looking directly at Nattie he added, "You are going to love this."

"Are you high?" asked Nattie.

"I'm not drunk, if that's what you mean."

To Charlotte Nattie asked, "I know it's not called manic depression anymore, but what do you call it when someone with his diagnosis gets on the high end?"

"It's still called mania. Mr. Moreland was diagnosed with bipolar II, so his highs are going to be hypomanic."

"Doctor Peppa explained that to you, didn't he, Nat?" asked Nathan, hovering over her.

"I want to hear from her if you don't mind," said Nattie firmly.

Nathan put his hands up in surrender as he took a step back. "Have you met the new shrink, Doc?" he asked Charlotte.

"If you need to pace, please do it over there," Charlotte said, pointing at an open area behind the conversational grouping they were sitting in. "Otherwise please sit back down."

Nathan sat back down. "He's real young looking," he said, and then he sang, "Dr. Pepper, for those who think young."

"That's a line from an old Dr. Pepper television commercial," explained Nattie.

"I think when he prescribes drugs he should call himself the 'quicker picker upper,'" continued Nathan.

"So is that the hypomania?" asked Nattie.

"Do you think you're manic now?" Charlotte asked Nathan.

Nathan looked down, scanning his body as if something might have grown, or shrunk, or changed. He patted himself lightly and said, "Can't I just be excited about something?"

"Do you have something to be excited about?" asked Charlotte.

"*Do I?*" he blurted. "I'll say I do."

"Can't he be both?" asked Nattie.

Nodding, Charlotte explained, "Not only can both hypomanic elation and celebration occur together, either can trigger the other. We just don't yet understand the way it works in you, Mr. Moreland. But we will."

Nathan sat at the edge of his seat looking like he could jump out of his skin any moment.

"Why don't you tell us why you're so excited?" suggested Charlotte.

Nathan nodded once, sat up straighter, and turned toward Nattie. "Do you remember that phone call when you hung up on me?"

Nattie blushed. To Charlotte she said, "He stood me up in front of my family. Then I didn't hear from him for weeks. That's when I find out his business has fallen apart. Then when he finally calls he wants me to invest my business in a wild scheme to hunt down international jewel thieves or something. As far as I can tell the only reason he got in touch with me then was because he needed me to do something he couldn't do because he was in jail." Glaring at Nathan, she said, "So, of course, I hung up. A smart woman would have hung up when she heard your voice."

"A smart woman might have listened to a no-risk business opportunity that had the potential to pull in a hundred thousand a year."

Nattie closed her eyes and shook her head slowly. Without looking in his direction she asked Charlotte, "Isn't grandiosity one of the symptoms of mania?"

"She doesn't have to answer that," interrupted Nathan. "You know very well that it is." To Charlotte he added, "I know it sounds far fetched, but the Federation Fidelity Insurance Company out of Chicago thinks I'm on to something. That's why I didn't call when I knew I was going to be late. I was on the phone making a deal with them." Back to Nattie, "They don't think I'm crazy."

They don't know you like I do, thought Nattie.

"That's the look she gets when she's not saying what she's thinking," Nathan said, explaining Nattie to Charlotte.

"I was *thinking* that when you turn on the charm, you could talk anyone into anything. Talking them into something doesn't prove anything. And for the record, I have never said I thought you were crazy."

Smirking, "Really?"

To Charlotte, "Okay, I probably did say that. But we were married, and I was mad. Never in connection to this stuff." To Nathan, "You deserved worse."

"Plenty worse, that's for sure. But for now, right now, what would it take for you to take me seriously?"

Nattie exhaled loudly.

"I think," interjected Charlotte, "that the task at this moment is to get your therapy—and Ms. Moreland's support of your therapy—off to a good start. I think expressing appreciation to her for being here is what this moment calls for. What do you think?"

Putting his hands up again, he responded, "My bad. I was so excited about what I'm trying to tell you that I forgot my manners. My mamma learned me better than that." He pivoted on the edge of his chair to face Nattie squarely. "I have disappointed you. I mean, I have failed you more times than I care to admit. And you have every right to kick me out of your life for good. I wouldn't blame you. Hell, no one in my family would blame you. So, when I tell you I know I don't deserve you being here, believe me I know it." A glance at Charlotte made him think of something else. "And I do appreciate it."

"I believe you, Nathan," said Nattie. She turned to Charlotte: "I do know he appreciates me. I'd go so far to say he depends on me." To Nathan she explained, "But that's not what I want from a husband, Nathan. I want someone I can depend on. Someone I can trust."

"I am going to be that guy. I know that I haven't been that guy, but I'm going to be that guy."

Nattie looked at him tenderly. "I don't know what to say, Nathan.

45

We had our chance. I still love you, and that's why I'm here. I want the best for you. But I don't see us ever getting back together."

"I know, Nattie. I know not to pressure you for anything more than a business association, and I won't. But I still want to know what it would take to get you to trust me enough for that."

Nattie hesitated.

"It does seem like a reasonable question," observed Charlotte. "You may not know how to answer it yet, but could you at least tell him you will consider how to answer?"

Nodding at Charlotte, then addressing Nathan, she said, "I can answer that right now." Pointing at him: "If you recover one of those insurance claims, that would go a long way to proving it's not just a pipe dream."

"So what am I supposed to do, pull a bag full of diamonds out of my pants?" he asked with a sarcastic edge.

Both women frowned until he stood up and pulled a small black felt bag from his pocket.

CHAPTER 11

Telling Lionel [Jack]

THE CONVERSATION SLOWED DOWN as our food began to arrive in waves. The only awkward moment came when Alice and I ordered wine and the O'Briens did not. Alice told me later that she hoped we had not offended them. Some Christians consider the consumption of alcohol to be a "bad witness" for their faith. Personally I consider legalism to be a "bad witness" for our faith, but as Alice has pointed out to me, "It is all just cultural practice. Not everyone who sounds legalistic is a sanctimonious zealot. And some of the sweetest-sounding people can be church killers and hunters of preacher scalps." For their part, the O'Briens did not seem to react one way or the other to our consumption. Besides, an all-the-alcohol-you-can-drink-included Sandals resort is not the place for a person offended by alcohol.

"What do you do for a living?" asked Lionel as we began dessert.

"I'm the building inspector for the city of Kingsport," I said. What I had planned on saying if someone asked me that question was, "Brain surgery, professional brain surgery." It was a line from the movie *Undercover Blues.* But when the golden opportunity to say it came, I didn't think of it.

"How about you, Lionel?" asked Alice. "What do you do?"

Ingrid put her hand on Lionel's forearm and leaned forward. I suppose that was a signal for him to let her answer for him, because he had started to open his mouth but closed it when she did that.

"Lionel is the O'Brien of the law firm O'Brien and Associates. I'm sure you've heard of them, right?"

"Why, yes," we both said, "of course." My response was a reflexive courtesy, but it must have been true if Alice said it.

Lionel laughed, "Thank you both for being so gracious." To Ingrid he said, "You put these nice people on the spot, dear. How are they supposed to respond to a question like that?"

"But I really have heard of your firm before," I assured him. I didn't explain that by the word "before" I meant that I had heard of his firm in the sentence immediately before the sentence when his wife had asked if we had heard of him.

"Oh, Jack," said Alice as her eyes lit up, "you should tell him about your summons."

"A summons," repeated Ingrid in a higher-than-normal pitch. "What's that about, Jack?"

"A summons just means he has to go to court. It could be about anything," explained Lionel. Leaning toward me, he asked, "You're not in trouble, are you?"

"He didn't do anything wrong," said Alice emphatically, "but he could still be in trouble, couldn't he? Tell him, Jack."

"Yes," agreed Ingrid, "tell him."

"Jack does not want to impose on me," Lionel told the women. "He knows this is my job and I'm on vacation." Then he turned back to me and added, "But it is my vacation, and I can do what I want. What I want right now is to hear why your lovely wife is so concerned. Give me the ten-minute version, and I'll tell you what I think. We mostly handle estate law, so this will be different for me."

Alice began before I could speak, "Some coins were found."

Lionel asked for a ten-minute version, and it generally takes Alice ten minutes to answer a yes-or-no question, so I knew I had to do something. I put my hand on her forearm and as apologetically as I could sound, I said, "It makes more sense for me to tell it."

"Do you remember that big art burglary in Kingsport about four years ago?" I asked them.

Lionel and Ingrid looked at each other, but neither showed any sign of recognition.

"It was the same night that the wolves escaped from Bays Mountain," added Alice.

The O'Briens both smiled and nodded their recognition, but all I could think was that's not part of the ten-minute version.

"On that same night there was a huge robbery. A lawyer named Presly Holmes had a safe room built in his house to store his art collection. Do you know him?"

Lionel nodded no.

I continued, "Someone just tore through one of the walls and cleaned it out."

"Someone," repeated Lionel. "They don't know who?"

"No," answered Alice.

"How much was taken?" asked Ingrid.

"Over four million, mostly paintings. I heard there was a Picasso, but I never saw it myself."

"And some gold coins," added Alice.

"Yes," I said, "there were gold coins, too."

"And those are the gold coins that someone just found," guessed Lionel.

"I assume so."

"If that is all it is, then there should be no problem for you," smiled Lionel. "They're probably going to use you to establish when and where the coins were found and ask you if you saw anything else. I wouldn't worry too much about it."

"But there is more to it," said Alice meekly.

All eyes turned toward her.

She hunched her shoulders up and looked a bit embarrassed. "Tell him you were the inspector."

"I was the building inspector," I repeated. "I was in and out of that job several times, but I had nothing to do with the construction of that safe room. During the trial the insurance company brought me in as a witness against the contractor. As far as I know I was never under suspicion."

"Oh, I'm sure you were considered," said Lionel in a matter-of-fact way, "but it bodes well that you didn't know. No one was convicted though, right?"

"I don't think so," I answered.

Lionel frowned as he looked down at his empty flan plate. The longer he kept quiet, the tighter Alice dug her nails into my hand. I guess she was concerned. "It's all just circumstantial, but if it were me I'd sure take representation with me when

I went. If you'd like me to, I can call the courthouse when we get back. Maybe I can find out if you are under suspicion. If you are, then I can recommend a good defense attorney if you need that."

"Hopefully he won't need it, right?" asked Alice.

"Absolutely," Lionel assured her. "It's probably nothing."

It didn't feel like nothing to me. Not anymore.

CHAPTER 12

The Black Bag

BOTH NATTIE AND CHARLOTTE WATCHED as Nathan moved a potted Easter lily from a small table under a window and placed it on the floor. He then placed the small table in front of his chair and sat down. He emptied the contents from the bag onto his palm and spread the little bag out on the middle of the table.

"Ladies," he announced, "feast your eyes on this." With that he spilled the contents of his palm out on the black felt bag. They remained speechless as he ran his index finger over the pile of stones, spreading them out.

"Are those diamonds?" asked Charlotte.

"Where did you get those, Nathan?" asked Nattie.

Laughing, Nathan observed, "Look who's manic now."

Neither woman looked particularly anxious at the moment. Both women were leaning forward, elbows on knees, transfixed.

Charlotte reached halfway to the diamonds before withdrawing her hand.

"Nathan, can you get into serious trouble having those?" asked Nattie.

"I'm okay," he said, leaning back in his chair. He crossed his legs and folded his hands behind his head. "I've already reported it to Kingsport PD. They know I've recovered this. They know I'm bringing it in. Federation Fidelity Insurance will cut me a check for forty thousand dollars as soon as they get confirmation from Kingsport."

Nattie sat back against her chair, a deer-in-the-headlights glaze across her face.

"You're witnessing a rare moment, Doc," Nathan said to Charlotte. "There's not many things that render her speechless."

"I think I'm a little speechless myself," admitted Charlotte. "It's not every day that someone throws a half million dollars on my end table."

"Technically it's only four hundred thousand," said Nathan.

"Really," said Nattie coming out of her stupor. "That's all you have to say? You're correcting her math?" She turned to Charlotte: "I'm sorry about the therapy, but I want to hear more about this. Is that okay?"

"I'm not sure what the therapeutic value is, but this is where the energy is and I don't see that changing, so let's go with it." Then to Nathan: "But may I suggest that you go ahead and pack up your fortune? I'm afraid one of us will kick that table and you'll lose one in my carpet."

Once Nathan had picked up all the diamonds, Nattie opened the bag for him.

With the bag stuffed back in his pocket Nathan returned the table to its spot under the window and placed the Easter lily back on top.

"Here's the quick version," he began as he sat back down. "I had already been talking to Federation Fidelity Insurance about retrieving dead claims for them when I got arrested." He held up his hand at Nattie, signaling for no comments. "The arrest turned out to be a lucky break because in the middle of the night they brought in another guy. He was only there an hour, and I pretended to be asleep the whole time he was there. But I heard everything that happened. He bribed a guard for the use of a cell phone. When the guard left he thought he was alone so he talked openly about their robbery of Baker's Jewelry in downtown Kingsport. His partner was supposed to meet a fence in Asheville but got scared when the fence didn't show. She hid the bag up inside those public chess tables by that little triangle park where they do the drum rounds. You remember where that is, don't you, Nat?"

Nattie nodded yes.

"Anyway, she got arrested for possession and was then expedited to Florida on another burglary charge. The next day is when I called you," pointing at Nattie. "I wanted to make sure one of us got there before either of them did." His face, which had been quite animated as he told his tale, became solemn. "I understand why you hung up on me. Believe me, I wanted to have all my ducks lined up before I talked to you, but I was worried about the timing." His face brightened again. "But it all worked out. It was easy to figure out who the insurer was. And after that it was just a matter of driving over to Asheville, grabbing the bag, and brokering a deal with Federation." He sat back. "That's all there was to it. Any questions?"

Nattie glanced at Charlotte. Seeing no signs of a question there, Nattie asked, "So, what happens when the real thief figures out you got his diamonds?"

"No problem. All he saw was the back of my head."

Nattie leaned forward. "Nathan," she began in her lower, let-me-explain-the obvious-to-you voice, "They are not going to let you return those diamonds and pay you without some sort of explanation of how you came by them."

His eyebrows knit together as he stared at her.

"They are going to wonder if you're the thief."

His eyes cleared.

"You're going to have to testify about what you heard and what you did."

Nathan shrugged. "Okay. That's what I'll have to do. It's part of the business, right?"

Nattie studied his face. She doubted he was up to the task of protecting himself if the need arose, and she was pretty sure it would arise. She also knew that if the need arose, she'd make it her responsibility, whether he could take responsibility or not.

"Oh, my," exclaimed Charlotte. "I'm afraid I have mismanaged the time. I'm late for my next appointment." As she stood she said, "It has been very . . . interesting, but now I must end. Please see Dyan on your way out."

They made another therapy appointment and headed out to the small parking lot adjacent to Charlotte Stevens's office together.

"Thanks for coming, Nattie. I mean it," he said, stopping well before they reached either of their cars.

"I know you do, Nathan. And I'm willing to do as much as I can to help you," she paused and narrowed her eyes before continuing, "as long as it's less than you."

He pulled his head back, a pained look on his face.

"I'm sorry," apologized Nattie, "that was awfully abrupt. All I want to say, and maybe it's just that I need to say it to me more than you, is that I'm determined to help you take care of you. I'm no longer willing to do more than you do when it comes to taking care of you."

His face relaxed. "Of course. That's how it should be."

"And Nathan."

"Yeah."

"You are going directly to Kingsport now, aren't you?"

"I'll be fine," he said almost singing.

She put her palm against the middle of his chest. "I'm serious, Nathan. That's a lot of money you have in that little bag. There are plenty of people who'd kill you for less."

"The only people who know about it are you and the Federation Fidelity people."

"And Charlotte," pointed out Nattie.

"Seriously," he frowned, "you think she's a threat?"

"Of course not. But I also think you can be way too casual about these sort of things."

"By 'casual' you mean 'sloppy,' right?"

Nattie sighed; she did mean "sloppy." "I just want you to be more careful."

He nodded his head forward with a bounce. "I hear you, captain." He left off the salute. After relaxing his shoulders he said, "Now, can I tell you about what's next?"

"I'm listening."

"Federation made a four-million-dollar payoff on an art burglary in Kingsport, and the art was never recovered."

"How long ago was the burglary?"

"Four years."

"And you think you're gonna do something that the cops and the insurance investigators didn't do back then?"

"I don't know everything I'm gonna do, but I've got three things going for me." He waited for her to ask, but he couldn't wait long. "First, to all of them it was a closed case for a year."

"It *was* a closed case," repeated Nattie.

"Yes, I said 'was,' but let me get to that in my own time."

Nattie turned her hand over several times, motioning for him to go ahead.

"Two," he said, holding up two fingers, "I've got you." Again he waited for a response from her and again he couldn't wait long. "At least I'm hoping I've got you on my team. This is potentially a four-hundred-thousand-dollar payout. You'd like half of that, wouldn't you?"

"I could figure out how to spend that, but I can't make a deal like that standing in a parking lot. Why don't you tell me what number three is, and then you can go get that thief magnet out of your pocket?

Call me tomorrow morning, and we can set up a time to figure out if we should try working together again. Okay?"

"Okay."

Prompting him Nattie said, "You said the case was closed. Is it reopened?"

"It is. Some of that stolen art collection finally turned up last week."

"What?" asked Nattie. "Around here?"

"Yeah," he said. "They found some gold coins up on Bays Mountain."

"That makes three," she nodded.

CHAPTER 13

Sunday Lunch

IT WAS HARDLY NOTEWORTHY THAT NATTIE'S STEPSISTER, Samantha, didn't approve of Knox. That much was easy to predict, but it was a bit out of character, even for Sam, that she was so bold about expressing it. It began when Knox arrived wearing her usual peasant blouse with the bare midriff while the rest of them, including Kevin, were wearing their summer go-to-church clothes. For the men, that meant long pants and a collared shirt. For the women, it meant a summer dress. When they gathered at the O'Brien home before church, Kevin explained that Knox would not be joining them for worship because she had a gig in Kingsport last night, but she'd try to get there for lunch.

Nattie and Samantha were helping Ingrid in the kitchen when the doorbell rang. Lionel and the men—Kevin; Elijah, Samantha's husband; and Trevor, their son—were hanging out in the den. Elijah and Lionel were discussing the merits of aluminum siding, so it was a race between Kevin and Trevor for the reprieve to answer the door.

Trevor, with younger and quicker legs, was the first to the foyer, so he drew the honors. Trevor had been present, in body but not mind, when the arrival of "Kevin's new girlfriend" had been discussed before church, so he was completely unprepared for what he saw when he opened the door. Knox, ever oblivious to the effect she had on men, smiled innocently at the eighth grader. Trevor, whose job it was to open the storm door, stood frozen, gazing unabashedly through the glass.

"Trevor," whispered Kevin from behind, "that's Knox. Open the door."

Trevor turned his head slightly and, still in a daze, looked at Kevin blankly. After a few seconds he shook his head and came out of his trancelike state. He turned beet red as he opened the door.

Knox glided past Trevor as she stepped through the open door. "Thank you."

Turning his head away from Knox, Kevin whispered into Trevor's ear, "Say 'hi.'"

"Ah . . . hi."

"This is my nephew, Trevor," said Kevin.

"Hi, Trevor," said Knox, standing too close for Trevor to breathe.

"Hello," said Lionel from the middle of the foyer. "I'm Lionel O'Brien, and this is Elijah Gorzilanski. I'm glad you could join us today."

"Thank you for inviting me," replied Knox, moving toward him with her hand extended. "You have a lovely home."

"Creature comforts," said Lionel as he took her hand.

"Hi," said Knox to Elijah as she offered her hand to him.

Elijah shook her hand and nodded his head once. He had even less to say than Trevor.

Lionel brought them all to the dining room where Samantha was placing a large serving of salad on the table.

"Sam, this is Knox," said Elijah as they entered the room.

As Samantha looked up, the "greet-people-at-church" smile disappeared. The words, "Oh, my," came out of her mouth involuntarily.

"Are you okay?" asked Nattie, who was bringing in a basket of sliced sourdough bread from Blackbird Bakery.

Samantha recovered her smile and circled the table. "Is that your costume?"

"I'm sorry," said a confused Knox.

"I think she wants to know if that's what you wear when you sing," explained Nattie, her voice droll.

"Why, yes it is," smiled Knox. "Thank you."

Nattie fought off a grin as she watched Samantha's face tighten. She had seen Knox's naiveté disarm people before, but this time was by far the most enjoyable.

"Knox," said Ingrid as she entered with a cauldron of Brunswick stew, "it's good to see you again." They had met at Nattie's office previously.

"It's good to see you, Mrs. O'Brien. Thank you for inviting me for lunch."

"Please, Knox," said Ingrid, setting the platter at the head of the table, "call me Ingrid." Then, looking up, she added, "Why are you all still standing?"

Lionel immediately lurched forward, gesturing Knox to the seat right next to him. "Please sit," he said, gesturing Knox to the seat to his left.

Kevin took the seat next to Knox with Nattie to his left. Samantha and her clan sat across from them, but when Elijah reached for his normal seat next to Lionel, Samantha slid in front of him. Elijah, confused for a moment, adjusted and redirected his son to the seat next to Ingrid where normally Samantha would have sat.

Nattie and her mother sent a did-you-see-that signal to each other with the briefest of eyebrow raises. *I'm glad someone else noticed that,* thought Nattie.

"Let's pray," announced Lionel as he held his open hands out to either side. Knox busied herself with coordinating holding hands with the men on either side of her so she missed Samantha's jaw dropping open. Other than Samantha's open mouth, no one else gave any indication that this was the first time they held hands during prayer.

The lunch conversation was predominantly focused on getting to know Knox. They wanted to hear about her music, her family, and eventually her church history.

"My family didn't really go to church much when I was growing up, but I went to Young Life camp my junior year," she explained.

"Young Life," repeated a perked-up Lionel. He had been a Young Life volunteer while he was in college and was currently on the Young Life Committee in Johnson City. "What camp did you go to?"

"I don't remember the name of it, but it's over near Asheville."

"Windy Gap," he told her.

"That sounds right," she said.

"Was it a good experience for you?" asked Ingrid.

"Oh yeah. It was great. I stood up the last night," she looked around the table. "Do you know what that means?"

"We do," said Lionel.

"It means you made a profession of faith," said Samantha. "Do you still believe what you said you believed that night?" Her tone was harsh and challenging.

The question brought a scowl from Lionel.

Knox shrugged. "I'm not sure if I understand everything that it means, but I think it means we can come to Jesus just as we are. When we got back from camp, all of us who stood up that night met with Matt every night for a while to study the Bible and to pray."

"Matt Richardson," said Lionel, "is the Young Life area coordinator in Bristol."

"I don't know about what he's called but he's the guy who took us and met with us. I still remember what he taught us about Nicorette, the wise man."

Samantha puckered her face.

"I think she means Nicodemus the Pharisee," said Kevin gently as he leaned toward Knox.

"He was a wise man," Lionel said without taking his eyes off Knox, which effectively cut Samantha off. "So tell us what you remember about Nicodemus."

"Matt said Nicorette, I mean Nicodermus, gets criticized all the time because he didn't come see Jesus the right way or something, but the important thing was that he did come."

"That's right," said Lionel. "I couldn't have said it better."

"It made me think," continued Knox, "that Jesus saw the real Nicoramus, not just the one everyone back then expected him to be. Him being a wise man and all, I think he was afraid to lose that."

"He was afraid to lose what?" asked Ingrid.

"His reputation," said Knox, looking down at her still half-full plate. "People must have respected him and that must have felt good, but he probably thought that people didn't really see him." She looked up at Lionel. "I just thought he was afraid he'd lose his reputation." She shrugged. "But I bet he knew his reputation wasn't really real any- way." Then she turned toward Ingrid. "That probably made going to Jesus even scarier for him."

Knox shrugged slightly and put her head down slowly.

Nattie wondered if Knox had been embarrassed by it all. Then Kevin put his arm behind her and gently stroked her back, which con- firmed it.

Lionel must have thought so, too, because he leaned against the table and softly said, "Knox, that was brilliant. How ever did you get all that out of that passage?"

Knox lifted her head and studied Lionel's face for a moment. Then with a glance toward Samantha she said, "Mostly people don't see me either."

CHAPTER 14

Carlton DeMarco [Jack]

ALICE TRIED TO COMFORT ME AS I LEFT THE HOUSE. "Don't be nervous. You didn't do anything wrong."

It did feel good to hear her say that as she walked me to the car. And the good feeling stayed with me as I drove through Bristol. I bought a coffee at AJ MoJo and nursed it while I listened to the David Crosby station on Pandora. But five miles out of town I finished the coffee and my thoughts began to drift.

By the time I got to the Kingsport city attorney's office, my stomach was in a knot. I told myself repeatedly that Alice was right; I didn't do anything wrong. But I also knew that no one else really knew I didn't do anything wrong. In Alice's case, she didn't really know I hadn't done anything wrong; she just believed it. For everyone else in the universe all I could say was that no one could prove I was guilty. As for Carlton DeMarco, the Kingsport City attorney, I had no idea what he thought, but I knew that he had no proof I was guilty either, at least not yet.

● ● ●

"Mr. Stout?" DeMarco asked when he walked over to where I sat in his waiting room.

He was a tall man with square shoulders, a tiny waist, and skinny legs. He was pale, he had no bulge over his belt, and his hand was clammy when I shook it. How am I supposed to trust a guy like that?

"I'm Jack Stout," I said. "Please call me Jack."

He led me down a hallway to a conference room. There was a manila folder on the table in front of the chair he stood behind. He pointed to the chair across from him as he sat down. "This is just an interrogatory." he said. "No reason to be nervous."

Is it that obvious, I wondered as I tried unsuccessfully to find something comfortable to do with my hands.

"I just need to ask you a few questions regarding some coins found on Bays Mountain."

"Am I a suspect?" I asked.

"A suspect?" he said, raising the pitch of his voice. "No one has mentioned a crime at this point, Mr. Stout."

Bull, I said to myself. "No one mentioned a crime," I said, "but I got a threatening note while I was on vacation demanding my presence here this morning, so let me ask you directly: Is there a crime that has not been mentioned?" I think I came off more aggressive than I intended. That meant I was even more frightened than I thought.

He studied me through narrowed eyes before smiling.

I wanted to slap that smile off his face.

"Something tells me that you already know the answer to that question, Jack."

"That's correct, I do."

"Frankly, Jack, I find that a bit curious." His syrupy voice carried the unspoken threat that if I didn't answer his questions, he'd assume I was guilty.

"Then I'd say it's a good thing you're not a cat." Sarcasm. Another symptom of fear.

His eyebrows knit together, which I took more as confusion than anger.

"You know what curiosity did to the cat?" I asked awkwardly trying to explain. *Get a grip,* I advised myself.

"Mr. Stout, is that a threat?" His voice was soft this time.

I felt a ping of guilt. "It was a play on words," I said. "If you were threatened then I offer my sincerest apologies." My fingers were comfortably crossed under the table. The apology was sincere even though it was coerced.

"Frankly, Jack, I find your resistance suspicious."

I stood up. "That's Mr. Stout, if you please. And I'm leaving." I was angry.

"I don't advise that."

I grinned. I'm not sure why I grinned, but I wasn't nervous anymore. "First you sent me a note demanding my presence. You didn't call me up and work out a mutually convenient time to meet. You told me when to come and I came. Then I asked you a straightforward question about whether or not I'm a suspect. According to my lawyer, I have a right to know the answer to that question. I have a right to know if I should have a lawyer present."

"Why would you think you need a lawyer?" he asked in the same syrupy voice he used to imply I was hiding something.

Ignoring his attempt to bait me this time, I continued. "It was a simple question and you have consistently avoided answering it, so I'm leaving."

"Suit yourself," he said matter-of-factly, then he opened the folder on the table and began writing.

As I swung open the door I heard him clear his throat.

"Please come back and take a seat, Mr. Stout."

Without letting go of the door I turned to face him. He was standing and holding his hand out toward my empty chair. The expression on his face was softer, even humble. "You're right, I was trying to push you."

I didn't let go of the door handle. "Am I a suspect?"

"You are officially not a suspect, but we are just beginning to decide whether to reopen the case."

I remained standing in the doorway. I felt like the balance of power had shifted in my direction, and I was going to enjoy it for a bit longer.

"You were involved with the original investigation four years ago, were you not?" he asked.

"Do you have the notes from that investigation?" I asked.

"I do."

"Then you already know that the contractor was the accused. I was called on as a witness."

He put his hands up, palms toward me, "I did know all that. I was just trying to get us on the same page." He pointed to my empty chair again. "Please, I promise this is just a preliminary interview. In the spirit of full disclosure I'll tell you this: there is a coincidence that has to be questioned and that is why you are here."

"Coincidence," I repeated.

"I'd sincerely like to eliminate you as a potential suspect."

Looking back now I realize there was no reason he should have wanted to cross my name off the suspect list and there was no reason I should have believed him. But I did. So I sat down across from him again.

"Here's the bottom line," he began. "You were the Kingsport building inspector four years ago when the Holmes robbery took place, correct?"

I nodded yes.

"And you inspected that safe room, right?"

"No," I said reflexively. It was a response that I had developed four years ago during the aftermath of that robbery. I was extremely sensitive about being blamed back then. My professional integrity was blemished by the whole affair. I was surprised that it still stung so much.

"No?" he questioned. "Did someone else do the inspection?"

I exhaled slowly and began to retell an explanation I had told many, many times before. "I inspected and approved the foundation and the structure of that room, but the manufacturer's specifications to make that a safe room were very detailed. The city manager directed me to avoid any connection to that part of the construction."

"Why would he do that?"

"I believe he talked to your predecessor about being sued. They had the homeowner sign a contract releasing the city of liability. Don't you have that document?"

"I'm sure we have it somewhere. I've never seen it, but I can track it down if need be." He jotted down something in the folder.

I watched but I couldn't read what he was writing.

He put his pen down and looked up. "Tell me about your relationship to Mr. Heart."

"I'd say our relationship was antagonistic."

"He was the contractor who built that safe room, correct?"

I nodded yes.

"And you and he were, what did you say, antagonists?"

"Yes. I'm sure he thought that I had it out for him."

"Why do you think that?"

"Well, for two reasons. The first is that he told me so on several occasions."

He started to write in his folder but lifted his head instead. "You said there were two reasons. What's the second reason?"

"It's true," I answered.

The confused look reappeared on his face.

"It was true that I was out to get him," I explained. "He was a cheat. I knew he was a cheat and he knew I knew he was a cheat. I wrote up warnings on him constantly, and he always knew just enough to do to avoid losing his license, but that makes him even more guilty in my mind."

"Please explain what you mean."

"He knew how to do it right when he knew he was in trouble, so when he didn't do it right it wasn't ignorance or a lack of skill."

"It was cheating," said Carlton, finishing my statement.

"Yes," I said. "It was cheating."

"And he was the chief suspect in the robbery case, was he not?"

"He was."

"But he was found not guilty of the robbery," said Carlton, tapping his folder. "Do you know why?"

"He was found not guilty, but I don't have a clue why. I remember thinking that it might be one more example of him playing fast and loose with the law, getting by on a technicality or a loophole."

"Have you had any contact with Mr. Avery since that time?" asked Carlton.

"No," I said. "If I remember correctly he got off the robbery charge, but the insurance company sued him for using inferior materials, which was his standard operating procedure."

"You knew he was going to do that," stated Carlton.

"I predicted it."

"To whom did you predict it?"

The question confused me. "What do you mean?"

"Who did you tell that you knew Mr. Avery would use inferior materials?"

The nervous feeling crept back into my stomach. "Are you asking me who else might have known that that safe room was not safe?"

He smiled.

"I told the city manager, and I'm pretty sure he told the city attorney, but beyond that, I'd be willing to bet that anyone who knew Heart Avery would have had the same thought as I did."

"I'm sure you're right," he said.

I watched him smile awkwardly at me from across the table. The image of a spider looking at his prey popped into my head. I felt a cold shadow pass through my belly.

"I think I should probably talk to my lawyer again," I said, as much to myself as to him.

"I think that's a good idea," he agreed.

CHAPTER 15

Pretty Girl Station

"PEACE AND GOODWILL," ANNOUNCED NATTIE as she crested the hill on State Street and downtown Bristol came into view. It was the way St. Francis greeted the morning, and it was the way she greeted her town.

It was midmorning when Nattie parked in front of her office across from Machiavelli's. Had she been in a hurry she'd have parked in front of Manna Bagel, but she wasn't in a hurry this morning. The three-block walk on State Street made her feel connected to Bristol, which seemed like it was changing faster than it should. Gone were the Grind House and CityMug. She'd spent many hours having coffee in each of them. As she walked she remembered the day the Sessions 27 music store sign was installed. Now Pretty Girl Station was where Sessions 27 used to be.

"Good morning, neighbor," called a voice from across the street.

Nattie turned to see who had called out and recognized Barbara, the owner of Pretty Girl Station, and Patty, the manager. They were standing under the boutique's awning. Patty, always with a big smile, was the one who had yelled. They both waved. Nattie waved back.

Nattie had first gone into Pretty Girl Station with Nathan. That was when it was at the mall. While she tried on a blouse, he bought her a necklace made from guitar strings. She told him she was happy with her St. Francis cross. He told her, "*You* can never be happy enough."

That's one of the problems with him, thought Nattie as she began walking toward Manna Bagel again. *All too often he says the right things.*

● ● ●

Having a Monday morning staff meeting at Manna Bagel was never official. It wasn't a decision made as a reaction to something gone wrong, as many decisions are. It was never deliberated, and it was never articulated. It just evolved.

"Your usual?" asked Brittney, the ever smiling blonde behind the counter.

Nattie's usual breakfast was an Early Bird Special with sausage on an everything bagel without cheese and a side of New Balance butter substitute. After fixing her coffee she joined Kevin at his window table.

"How was your weekend?" he asked as she sat down.

"I pulled an all-nighter on Friday night, so I was pretty much a zombie for the rest of the weekend."

"Did you get the pictures you needed?"

"I did."

"Well, that was nice and fast," he observed.

"It's always is when they're guilty."

Brittney brought Nattie's breakfast to the table. The bagel had been sliced but the sandwich had not been cut in half like normal. Nattie had forgotten to say not to cut it. "Thanks for not cutting it," said Nattie.

Brittney smiled. "Anything else?"

"Yeah," said Nathan, who had come unnoticed through the back entrance. "I'd like one of those, too."

Brittney stepped to the side to escape being in the middle. "Do you want it just like hers?"

"Absolutely," he said. Then he pointed back and forth between Nattie and Kevin. "Refills anyone?"

Both shook their heads no.

As soon as Nathan, who was following Brittney back to the counter, got out of earshot, Nattie leaned across the table. "What's he doing here?"

"I suppose he's hungry," said Kevin.

She glared at him.

"Okay," Kevin said with a shrug, "he called this morning and asked if we still had our Monday morning staff meeting at Manna."

"And you told him yes."

"Of course. Why wouldn't I?"

"Because I have not decided how much of my life I am going to let him in on."

Kevin leaned back.

Nattie wondered, *Are you getting out of arm's reach?*

"What's the problem, Sarge? This is just a staff meeting, not a date. Besides, isn't he your new partner?"

"Did he tell you that?"

"He said he had a twenty-thousand-dollar check for you as part of a diamond robbery. That pretty much seems like you're partners." As he said this, his eyes moved to Nattie's left.

She turned just as Nathan reached the table. He had to drag a chair from another table in order to sit. "So, how was your weekend?" he asked.

"You know how it is," she said. "Work-recover-work-recover."

"She pulled an all-nighter," explained Kevin.

Nathan nodded toward Kevin, and then, turning to Nattie, he asked, "Don't you hate that part of PI work?"

"Yes, but it pays the bills."

Nathan lifted his eyebrows. "Won't it be nice when you don't need to worry about paying the bills?"

"And when would that be?" she snapped back a bit quicker than she intended.

"When he gives you a check for twenty grand," guessed Kevin.

She gave Kevin a look that said, "You don't have to leave, but don't be here."

"I do, or at least I will, have a check for twenty thousand for you. That last recovery got me a forty T payoff, and I told them this morning to write a check to you for half."

"You don't need to do that, Nathan. Ten percent is all I asked for."

"Well, half is what I want you to have." He quickly held up his hand to stop her from objecting. "But it's also what has to happen. The primary payout has to be to an agency, so 50 percent is the least that they will go for."

She studied him. She wasn't sure how she knew, but she was sure there was more to tell. She waited.

"The next job could have a payoff ten times this one," he stated.

"Four hundred thousand," said Kevin out loud.

Nathan smiled as if he had accomplished something.

"What else do they require, Nathan?" asked Nattie.

"They need a secure fax line to send documents to, and you'll need to sign some confidentiality documents."

"We've got a secure fax line," stated Kevin. "They can send the papers today."

Nattie lowered her voice, "What else?"

"They need something documenting that I'm an employee and that I'm the authorized representative of the Natasha McMorales Detective Agency."

"I see," she said before turning her full attention to her breakfast.

She knew both men were waiting for her to respond, and she knew they were watching her eat. The attention had the effect of slowing her down. Her bites were smaller, they were chewed longer, and there was wiping of her mouth and a sip of coffee between each bite.

The silence was broken when Brittney returned with Nathan's sandwich, which was in a takeout bag.

"Well," said Nathan.

"Well," Nattie said slowly, "give them the fax number, and when the paperwork comes I'll look at it, but I'm not committing to anything yet."

Nathan grinned. He stood up and bent over her in an attempt to kiss her forehead.

Jerking her head back she said, "There'll be none of that. I'm not sure what all this is. I'm not even sure *if* this is, but it's definitely not a courtship."

He backed off. "I'm sorry. It won't happen again. I was just excited that we'll be working together again."

"I didn't say that," she said firmly.

"I know you didn't say it," he said as he picked up his bag. "I was listening to the music."

Nattie watched him leave. "He was listening to the music," she repeated, shaking her head.

"I think he was referring to that," said Kevin, pointing at her throat.

She was surprised. When she looked down she discovered that instead of putting on her usual St. Francis cross she had opted for the necklace Nathan had given her.

CHAPTER 16

The Bagel Exchange [Jack]

LIONEL O'BRIEN WAS SITTING OUTSIDE THE BAGEL EXCHANGE when I arrived. He looked perfectly at ease in a navy blue suit, white dress shirt, and pale blue silk tie. Had I been dressed that way, I would have constantly fidgeted with my collar and there would have been no way I could have sat down and stood back up without dislodging my dress shirt from my pants. On Lionel, everything stayed where he had put it. It must be nice.

"Hi, Lionel," I said as I got close to his table. "Thanks for meeting with me."

He quickly closed the file he was reading and stood up. Extending his hand, he responded, "Good to see you, Jack. Glad to help." He pointed down the street. "I have to be at the courthouse this morning, so this was no problem at all. Do you want a coffee or something?"

"I'm good," I said.

He pointed to the chair next to him and sat back down. "So, Jack, tell me, what's happening with your summons?"

"I met with the city attorney, Carlton DeMarco. Do you know him?"

Lionel shook his head no.

"Basically, they are going to reopen that robbery case from four years ago, and I think I might be a suspect now."

"Did he say that?"

"No, not really, but he got me to say that I knew that safe room wasn't built right and was vulnerable to a robbery."

Lionel rubbed his chin. To me it looked like he was slowing himself down, making sure to carefully consider what he heard before speaking. It was not what he looked like when we were having dinner together in St. Lucia.

"Is that new information?" he asked.

"Not really. In my deposition during the original investigation I told them that it was common knowledge that the contractor would cut any corners he could get away with."

"That doesn't incriminate you any more now than it did then," observed Lionel. "So what difference would that make now?"

"He got me to say that I predicted the robbery."

"This, of course, doesn't prove your innocence, but why would you have predicted it if you were going to do it?"

"He seemed pretty interested in who I predicted it to."

"And who was that?"

"The then city manager and city attorney."

Lionel nodded. "Maybe he's after one of them."

"Maybe," I shrugged, "but they're both dead."

He smiled. "That doesn't prove innocence either."

I must have looked more worried than I thought because he leaned toward me and said, "It's probably nothing, Jack. Sometimes prosecutors like to just push somewhere to see what happens. It usually means they don't have a better plan in mind." He tried a comforting smile. "I tell you what. If this goes to court, which I really, really doubt, I've got a guy in my office who does a lot of trial work in Kingsport. He's already familiar with the Holmes robbery case, and when I told him about

75

those coins and you getting a summons he said, "If they pursue it based on that, we'll have a wrongful prosecution case.'"

"I don't want to sue anybody. I just don't want it to go that far at all."

"One thing you could do is hire your own detective to find out who did it." He sat back. "If we can prove someone else did it, it's over."

"Can we do that? Hire a cop?" I asked.

"No, you can't hire a policeman, but you can hire a private investigator. I know a PI in Bristol I can recommend, but really, Jack, I believe it's a totally unnecessary expense."

Normally the phrase "unnecessary expense" would be enough of a deterrent, but this was an extraordinary thing for me. "What's his name?" I asked.

He handed me a business card. "First of all, it's a her not a him, and second, in the spirit of full disclosure I want you to know that I know her."

I looked at the card. It said "The Natasha McMorales Detective Agency." "What kind of a name is that?"

"That's just the name of the agency," he explained. "Her name is Natalie Moreland."

"And she's the best in the area?" I asked.

"She is," he told me without any hesitation at all.

His quick answer made me feel good. "And you've used her before." I just said this out loud. It wasn't a question. I just assumed he was so high on her because she had worked for him.

"Not exactly," he said. This time his answer was not so inspiring.

I looked up from the card.

"She's my daughter," he told me.

CHAPTER 17

Federation Fidelity

NATTIE LOOKED UP FROM BEHIND HER DESK to see Nathan standing in the middle of her office. It was Thursday afternoon. She hadn't seen nor heard from him since Monday morning. She hadn't expected to, either. He was holding an oversized manila envelope and grinning.

She was on the phone, so she held up her index finger signaling to give her a minute.

He laid the envelope on her desk and left her office to join Kevin and Knox at the reception desk.

"Another houn' dog to sniff out?" asked Nathan when Nattie emerged from her office.

"What's a houn' dog?" asked Knox.

"An unfaithful husband," explained Nattie. She handed a folded sheet of paper to Kevin. "See what you can find out about this guy."

Kevin unfolded the paper and read the name.

"A houn' dog?" asked Nathan again.

Kevin refolded the paper and put it in a drawer. "Houn' dogs are good for cash flow," he told Nathan.

"Is there a special name for an unfaithful wife?" asked Knox.

"We used to call them 'Janes' because they always seemed to be married to Tarzans, but we don't do that anymore because the last Jane we had was really named Jane and she was married to an ape," explained Kevin.

"What's this?" asked Nattie, holding up the manila envelope.

"That's—" began Nathan pointing at the envelope, "your ticket out of the houn' dog business."

Nattie fought off the temptation to roll her eyes. To Kevin she asked, "Is my schedule clear for a while?"

Kevin immediately gave her a thumbs-up.

Tipping her head toward her office Nattie said, "Let's see what you have."

"Do you want all of us?" asked Kevin.

Nattie turned and did a slow scan of the crew before her. *What a group,* she thought. *Not exactly the League of Extraordinary Gentlefolk, but what did I expect?* "Yes," she said, "I want all of us."

"Even me?" asked Knox.

"Of course," answered Nattie. "You've got a knack for noticing things and connecting them in a different way than any of the rest of us. I'm counting on that."

A smile traced across Knox's face as she glanced at Kevin. She was the first to follow Nattie into her office.

Nattie sat behind her desk. In front of her were two pads of paper, one red and two blue pens, and the manila envelope.

Knox sat cross-legged and sideways in one of the upholstered chairs facing Nattie's desk. Dressed in short denim shorts and a baggy green T-shirt she looked like she was waiting for a slumber party to start.

Nathan sat in the other upholstered chair. He was wearing a pink polo shirt and khaki pants, looking like he was waiting for a frat party to start.

Kevin rolled the chair from his desk in and set up on the other side of Nathan facing Knox. He looked more like he wanted to be alone with Knox than to be at any sort of party.

"Okay," began Nattie, "catch me up on our relationship with Federation."

Nathan looked confused, but Kevin knew right away what she was asking. "Nathan forwarded me all the paperwork on Monday after we talked at Manna, so I got all that taken care of that afternoon. That stuff," he jutted his chin toward the envelope on the desk, "was couriered here late yesterday. It was marked 'Attention Nathan Moreland,' so I called him to let him know it was here."

"Thank you, Kevin," said Nattie. "So I'm in business with Federation Fidelity now, right?"

"We have a business relationship now that does not obligate you to do anything other than handle their case files with the same professionalism you handle any of your other clients," answered Nathan.

"That's a no-brainer," offered Kevin quickly.

Nattie eyed him before saying, "It is a no-brainer. I've got no problem agreeing to do exactly what I'm going to do anyway. What I have a problem with is the two of you conspiring together."

Nathan's head flinched back. His hands spread out before him as he asked, "What does that mean?"

"I'm not really speaking to you, Nathan."

All eyes turned to Kevin.

"Me?" he exclaimed. "What did I do?"

"You have become very quick in your support of anything that comes from Nathan."

Kevin raised his eyebrows and held his hand on his chest. "I'm quick to support good ideas. He's really on to something big here." He looked at Nathan.

"Thanks, Kevin," said Nathan. To Nattie he added, "This is a great opportunity, Nat. I wish you were more enthusiastic about it, but I understand." To Kevin Nathan said, "She has a right to be suspicious."

Kevin put up his hands in mock surrender. "Okay, okay. I'll keep my two cents to myself."

"Don't pout," ordered Nattie, not that he was really pouting. "When we are brainstorming about the case, I'm going to want every two-cent idea you have. Just don't try to sell him to me. Okay?"

"Got it," answered Kevin.

After a moment of silence Nattie asked, almost rhetorically, "Am I being too harsh?"

"Just a little bit," answered Knox.

That anyone answered the question was a surprise. That it was Knox was more so.

Nattie looked at Knox. She still looked like she was waiting for a slumber party to start, but her eyes met Nattie's eyes without flinching.

"I'll do better," Nattie told her.

CHAPTER 18

The Report

NATTIE TURNED HER ATTENTION TO THE ENVELOPE in her hands. For the first time she noticed that the top had been sliced open. "Have you already gone through all this?" she asked Nathan.

"I have," he told her as she removed the contents from the envelope.

She placed the contents in a pile in front of her and announced what the items were as she worked her way through the pile. On top were copies of the insurance policies, including a detailed list of the collection. Next came several documents from the Kingsport Police. Finally came several reports from the Federation Fidelity investigator, each one focusing on individuals deemed potential suspects.

"Okay, Nathan," said Nattie, when she finished listing the contents. "Why don't you give us the *Reader's Digest* version of the original robbery?"

"Presly and Ginger Holmes had an extensive art collection," began Nathan. "Instead of storing it somewhere safe, they decided to build a safe-room addition onto their house. A month after the safe room was finished, it was broken into, and all the contents were stolen. Federation Fidelity paid four-point-five mil."

That was certainly the Reader's Digest *version,* thought Nattie as Nathan finished. "Tell us more about the break-in."

"It was pretty simple really. Someone tore a hole in the side of the house, all the way down to the studs, and then they pushed the wall boards in and cut out one stud. After that it was just a matter of walking everything out through the hole. There were tire tracks backed up to the spot, so they hauled everything away in one move."

"What about the electricity?" asked Kevin.

"There wasn't any," answered Nathan.

"There wasn't any?" repeated Kevin in a higher pitch.

"The electricity was knocked out that night because of a power failure."

"That's convenient," said Knox.

The abruptness of Knox's comment caught everyone off guard. Knox's head slunk down a bit as the others shifted their attention toward her.

"Go on," Nattie told Knox.

"When you consider we only have blackouts a couple of times a year at the most, then it's quite a coincidence, isn't it?" said Knox.

"And it could be a coincidence," stated Nattie, "but what does it mean if it isn't?"

"It means someone had to be prepared when it happened," said Kevin.

"So they had to be ready to go, truck and all, when the power went," added Nathan.

Nattie began writing notes. She wrote "truck—size?" Then as she wrote "tools?" she asked, "What kind of tools were needed to get through a wall like that?"

"I'm not sure," said Nathan. "Nothing fancy, though. Pry bars, an axe, and some kind of saw would be enough."

She crossed the word "tools" off her list. "So we're not necessarily looking for someone with special tools."

"Not necessarily," agreed Nathan.

"Wouldn't using an axe make a lot of noise?" asked Kevin.

"Probably, but the house is sitting on four wooded acres, so no neighbor is going to hear or see anything anyway," replied Nathan.

"What about the people in the house?" asked Knox.

"All gone."

"Another convenient coincidence," said Nattie, looking at Knox, who nodded agreement. Then Nattie raised another question: "How long would it take to break through a wall like that and then load a truckload of artwork?"

"I'm guessing maybe an hour to break through and another hour to transfer everything to a truck," guessed Nathan.

"Maybe two hours," said Kevin, "if we were talking about breaking through a regular wall with no regard for making noise or ruining anything, but this isn't a normal wall. This room was supposed to be built like a safe. Those walls would have been wired even if the power was off, and what about the walls?"

"What about the walls, Kevin?" asked Nattie.

"It was a safe," he said. "That's like a bank vault. You can't just punch in the side of a vault. It would have some kind of steel reinforcement or something like that."

"You said it right when you said it wasn't supposed to be like a regular wall," said Nathan, "but that's a huge part of the story. The walls weren't like a safe. They were just regular walls. And the only place the electronics were installed was the front door."

"So the contractor did it," stated Kevin, tapping his finger on his palm and leaning back like he was finished with this mystery and was waiting for his praise.

"That's what everyone thought at first, but they couldn't connect the contractor to the crime. He was at the IRS office in Nashville at the time, so his alibi is pretty solid." "Let's not get ahead of ourselves," said Nattie. "I know this guy is going to be one of our suspects, but let's keep our focus on the crime for a while. Now, Nathan, did you say there were no electronics installed in the wall that was broken in?"

"Yes."

"Then the blackout doesn't really matter," said Kevin.

"We don't know what the thief knew or didn't know," said Nattie. "They may have thought the blackout was important, even though it wasn't. The important information may have been that the homeowners were gone that night." She recited out loud as she wrote, "We're going to want a list of who knew about the faulty construction and who knew that the house would be empty that night."

"Was anything ever recovered?" asked Kevin.

"Not much," said Nathan.

"Didn't you tell me some coins were just found?" asked Nattie.

"Yes," Nathan said, almost strutting. "Some coins were found up on Bays Mountain about a month ago."

"Coins don't have serial numbers like currency, so how do they know they're from that burglary?" asked Kevin.

"You're right," admitted Nathan. "We can't know for sure, but these were gold proof coins from the mint. There were three of them, and one had Martha Washington on it."

"Is that what a collectible is?" asked Knox.

"It is," Nattie told her as she looked through the itemized list until she came to what she was looking for. "There were twenty coins from something called 'The First Ladies Series.'"

CHAPTER 19

The Suspects

"WE'RE LOOKING FOR SOMEONE," Nattie held up a finger, "who had knowledge about the room full of valuables." Holding up a second finger she went on, "Had access to at least a small truck." Holding up a third finger, "Had the equipment and physical wherewithal to break through a wall and move a truckload of art in a single night." She looked around the room. "Anything else?"

"Knew about the faulty construction," said Nathan.

"Probably," agreed Nattie.

"And knew about the house being empty," offered Knox tentatively.

"Likely," responded Nattie.

"Let's look at the suspects in the packet," suggested Nathan.

"Let's brainstorm our own list first," said Nattie.

"The contractor," said Nathan.

"I don't think it's him," said Knox.

"I'm curious, Knox. How come?" asked Nattie.

"I don't know," said Knox. "I just figured that if he was going to come back and rob the place later, he wouldn't have been so obvious about making it wrong. He would have gone to more trouble to make it look right, and he would have just left a seam only he would know about." She shrugged. "You know, instead of leaving all the wiring out, he could have left the wiring out of one specific spot in the wall, then when he broke in, he could have cut that chunk out, making it a mystery how he got around the electronics."

"That's not how electrical systems work," said Nathan. "You can't just have a bad chunk, because the circuit has to be complete or it wouldn't have worked at all."

"The system didn't work at all," said Kevin.

"True," agreed Nattie, "but we can't rule the contractor out on the basis of what he would have done if he was as clever as Knox." To Knox she added, "That was a good thought, though."

"There's the homeowners," said Nathan.

"And we should think of them separately and together," added Nattie. "Who else would have known about the faulty construction?"

"There's whoever worked on the site," said Nathan.

"And anyone who delivered supplies to the site," added Kevin. "They may have known what was going into that room."

"Anyone else?"

"The building inspector from the city," answered Nathan.

"The building inspector," repeated Nattie. "I forgot about that. He must have signed off on all the faulty work."

Nathan let a little giggle escape as he rubbed his hands together. "This is starting to get fun," he announced.

"What about the empty house?" asked Nattie. "Who knew about that?"

"The homeowners, of course, plus friends, neighbors, and anyone who worked there," rattled Kevin.

"Was there a housekeeper?" asked Nattie.

"I don't know," said Nathan.

"We'll need to track down who would have known about the comings and goings of the homeowners," said Nattie as she wrote another note. "Shall we look at suspects now?" Nattie asked, as she picked up the first suspect report from the insurance company. "Avery Heart," she read.

"That's the contractor," said Nathan. "He was their primary suspect, but they couldn't prove anything other than he was derelict in his duties."

"Accomplices?" asked Nattie.

Nathan shrugged. "He was brought in for questioning but never charged. The report doesn't mention possible accomplices, but I'll check that out."

"Is he still in business around here?" asked Nattie.

"The insurance company sued him for breach of contract, but he declared bankruptcy. The whole thing cost him plenty, though. He lost his license, and the bankruptcy suit brought even more scrutiny from the IRS, which got him some prison time, which he is still serving up in New Jersey. His wife moved to the DC area. I've got an address where she works."

Nattie held up the second page. "Presly Holmes," she read.

"The homeowner," said Nathan. "He was a prime suspect, too. He's a lawyer in Kingsport. He was married to Ginger George. Her father owns half the fast-food restaurants in Kingsport. They're divorced now. The reason Federation Fidelity considered him such a prime suspect was because of how the insurance policy was so specifically written."

"Go on," said Nattie.

"The art should have been marital property, but the insurance policy was worded so that he would be the sole payee."

"Is that why they divorced?" asked Nattie.

"I don't know, maybe."

Nattie asked, "Was he questioned by the police?"

"I don't know that either, but he was questioned by the insurance investigator on the night of the robbery. He spent the evening at a black-tie affair at the Meadowview Conference Center. He left near midnight and went straight to the police station. He had to arrange bail for some guy and was there until nearly five o'clock. He had motive, but his alibi is pretty airtight, too." Nathan paused, "According to the insurance dick, he was in plenty of security footage at both Meadowview and the police station."

"He could have accomplices, too, right?" asked Kevin.

"He and the contractor could be in on it together even," offered Knox.

"We'll want to check all that out," said Nattie as she lifted the next page. "Ginger Holmes."

"The wife," said Nathan. "She was in Europe at the time and she had no motive. They checked out her alibi and moved on."

"We'll want to talk to her," said Nattie.

"And the last one," she said as she lifted the last page, "is Alexander Sebastian Stout."

"Alexander Sebastian Stout," repeated Kevin, "What an ass." No one laughed. Nattie scowled at him. He smiled sheepishly and said, "Sorry."

"He's the building inspector in Kingsport," said Nathan. "They originally considered him a possible suspect because they assumed he had okayed the shoddy construction. But that was not the case. He signed off on the footing and foundation only. The city's investigation took quite a lot of Mr. Stout's testimony. Apparently he didn't care much for the contractor, and he was not shy about saying so. Eventually they didn't consider him much of a suspect because instead of covering up Mr. Heart's faulty work, he was quite vocal about it."

"To whom?" asked Nattie.

"To the homeowner, the city manager, and the city attorney."

Nattie looked down at her notes. "Well, at least we don't have a shortage of suspects." She looked up at Nathan. "You've got the contractor, right?"

He nodded yes.

"I'll take Mr. Holmes," she continued. "Kevin, I want you to do backgrounds on all these folks, but start with Holmes and Heart."

CHAPTER 20

Micah [Jack]

IT WAS IMMEDIATELY COMFORTING when Lionel told me, "It's probably nothing." But that was several days ago, and the comfort value of his words was waning. I still hadn't told Alice about either the conversation with Lionel or the one with the city attorney. She knew about the summons and she knew I was nervous about it, so I had expected she'd ask me about it when I got home. I didn't want to talk about it anyway, so when she didn't ask, I let it be.

Maybe she didn't ask because her mind was on something else. Maybe she was so focused on our grandson's upcoming visit that it slipped by her. His parents, from Asheville, North Carolina, were leaving their toddler, Micah, with us while they went to a wedding in Sevierville. Whatever the reason, I was pleased with the reprieve. Being with Carlton DeMarco upset me. Being with Lionel calmed me down. And now, when the house was full of relatives, I was getting ramped up again.

Don't get me wrong. I love my kids, and I love having them around. I just don't like being in trouble. I don't like the *threat* of being in trouble any better. I never have. I could never be a criminal. If I was guilty,

I'd worry myself sick looking over my shoulder. The only times I've ever been in trouble, I was innocent.

There was that time in the fourth grade when a kid from a third-grade class came in and pointed me out from the front of my class. They took me in the hall, and his teacher accused me of picking this kid up and hanging him off a fence. The kid's mother wanted justice done, and she wanted the guilty kid to pay for the torn shirt.

"I didn't do it," I told them, and my teacher, Miss Farquar, believed me.

"If he says he didn't do it, he didn't do it," she told the other teacher.

It was a bizarre experience for me. I really didn't believe I had done it, but for the rest of the week a number of the other fourth graders claimed they had seen me do it. It was so bad that I began to wonder if I was crazy. I knew I didn't remember doing it, but I began to question my memory, which was a short step from questioning my sanity.

It was also bizarre because of what Miss Farquar had said. She had defended me on the basis that I wouldn't lie. I came to love that she believed in me like that, because I knew better. I knew that I'd have lied in a heartbeat to get out of trouble.

The fear of being in trouble has stayed with me, but so has Miss Farquar's belief in me in spite of the evidence. When I was in high school I went to a church camp with my friend Teddy Little. The speaker told us about Jesus every night after dinner, but the talk that really stuck with me was the night he said, "God loves you in spite of the evidence." That sentence made sense to me. I had experienced it before.

● ● ●

Alice and I turned in early that night. Tending to an energized two-year-old for three days wore us out. That may be the worst part of aging, because two-year-olds are my favorite humans. Their sense of wonder at everything they discover is a joy to behold. By the time they turn two and a half they'll start having spontaneous meltdowns because they can't do all the things they watch others do, and they get furious. Alice says in that way they are like old men. But she's biased.

As much as I love being with Micah when I'm with him, I also love sleep after being with him. Alice is the same. So it was no surprise to find us in bed before ten o'clock that night.

"He's cute as a bug, isn't he?" I told her as I nestled into my pillow. I wonder where that phrase came from; "cute as a puppy" would make more sense.

"He is," she said, "and he knows it."

"Maybe so, but he can pull it off. Remember when he did the little marionette dance while you were trying to get him to eat his green beans?"

"He was playing to you then," she told me. "He wasn't looking at me." Then, in a voice that was supposed to be Micah's alter ego, she added, "Look at me, Grandpa—see what I can get away with while I'm wearing diapers."

"He'll only get away with that for another few months," I said, "but I'll be wearing diapers and getting away with things long after he can't anymore."

She let me enjoy my cleverness far too briefly before saying, "Don't count on it." She kissed me lightly on the end of my nose. I guess she was still feeling maternal.

"Are you ready to talk about it?" she asked.

"Talk about what?"

"Talk about what's been bothering you since your court appearance, Grandpa."

"It wasn't really a court appearance," I began to explain until she bonked me on the forehead with the palm of her hand. "Okay, I'll talk. It shook me up."

"Are you in trouble?"

"I don't know. I talked to that lawyer from Johnson City we met in St. Lucia."

"The socks guy?"

"Lionel O'Brien," I told her. "He doesn't think I have anything to worry about. He thinks this DeMarco guy is just trying to shake the tree to see what falls out, but it still shakes me up."

She grinned. I couldn't believe it.

"I can't imagine why I was hesitant to talk," I said in my snottiest seventh-grade voice.

"Did you hear what you said?" she asked. She didn't wait for an answer. "You said, 'It shakes me up to be shaken.'"

That didn't really make me feel better, but her next kiss, which wasn't maternal at all, did.

"Besides," Alice said, "Lionel gave you some options, didn't he?"

"He did. He says he's got a lawyer who's ready to do a countersuit if it comes down to it."

"You see?" she said.

"Wait a minute. How'd you know what he told me?"

"Ingrid called me to check on you. I guess she and Lionel talk."

I decided to pretend I didn't catch that last remark.

"She said," continued Alice, "that the detective he told you about is the best detective in the area."

"Did she tell you that she's Lionel's daughter?"

"Actually, she's Ingrid's daughter from her first marriage."

The thought of hiring a detective had been on my mind ever since Lionel suggested it. I felt like a Ping-Pong ball bouncing back and forth between the fear of being in trouble and the possibly unnecessary expense of hiring a detective.

"I don't know about hiring a PI," I confessed. "That makes it all seem more real than I want it to be."

"But it might make you feel better," she suggested. "At least you'd be doing something."

"I don't know."

"Look," she said, snuggling closer to me, "if it keeps you from worrying yourself sick, then it's worth it." She was so close now that I could watch her eyes move from one of mine to the other. "That's the hang-up, right? The expense?"

"Of course," I admitted. There was no reason to pretend it wasn't true.

"Well, do you even know how expensive it would be?"

"No."

"You could call her and ask."

"I will," I said, in a voice that even I didn't believe.

"Or you could ask her yourself over lunch on Sunday."

This news perked me up. "Lunch," I repeated.

"We're having lunch with the O'Briens next Sunday."

I don't know why I don't want to talk about money. Maybe it's a part of being cheap. Maybe it's a part of being an avoider of conflict. Maybe my mother was frightened by a banker when I was in the womb.

"Since you and Ingrid get along so well . . . ," I began in a whiny, little-boy voice.

"You want me to talk to her," finished Alice.

I smiled a little-boy, I-know-you-caught-me-but-aren't-I-cute smile. It's a smile that almost always works on her. I try not to overuse it, but so far it has been my lucky charm.

Alice held up her finger. "I'll talk to Ingrid for you but not until after you check her daughter out on Sunday."

"Thanks," I said.

Alice nodded her head in acknowledgment and then closed her eyes.

Who needs a diaper? I thought.

CHAPTER 21

Nathan Calls

"WHERE ARE YOU NOW?" ASKED NATTIE. It was Wednesday afternoon. Nathan had left early Monday morning for the DC area. His information put Avery Heart's wife, Shannon, working at the Mount Vernon historical site. Attempts to trace her through a real estate purchase did not turn up an address. If she or Avery had bought property, their names would have shown up. With the only lead being a place of employment, Nathan's plan was to go there and wait. Employers would normally frown upon someone hanging around loitering, but at a location like Mount Vernon, Nathan just looked like another tourist wandering around appearing interested or lost.

"Right now I'm standing on the lawn in front of George's house. Did you know it's made out of wood but carved and sandblasted to look like stone blocks?"

"No, I didn't. Have you found out anything else?" she asked trying for level-three sarcasm.

"Well, I found out that George liked ice cream and it took them hours to make it for him."

"Anything else?" she asked, this time trying for level-six sarcasm.

"He had a distillery, and he invented a process to thresh grain with horses in an eight-sided barn."

"Well," she said, hitting a ten this time. "I see you've had a great field trip. I have work to get back to, so I'll wait for the rest of your report when you finish your shadowbox."

"I had lunch with her," he said hurriedly.

"With Mrs. Heart?"

"Actually, it's the ex–Mrs. Heart. She's not paid here; she's a volunteer. I got here on Monday afternoon and she wasn't working, but on Tuesday I found her at the blacksmith shop. I asked a lot of questions about the history here. It is pretty fascinating, so she thought I was just another tourist. Then today I just happened to eat lunch at the same time as she did."

"Interesting," said Nattie. Deception was not her normal methodology. It was her belief that the best way to keep the flow of information going was to be honest and genuine. Deceiving someone might get some information from them, but when the manipulation was discovered, the flow of information would inevitably run dry.

"I acted like I was interested in becoming a volunteer like her and wanted to hear her story."

"So what did you find out?"

"According to Shannon, her husband was a scoundrel who made and then lost a lot of money. He's still in jail for tax fraud, which left her dependent on her son, who is a historian employed at Mount Vernon. That's why she moved there and why she volunteers there."

"Is there any possibility that she has some money he may have squirreled away from that robbery?"

"I don't know," he answered. "She said that he lost everything they had, but at least he didn't leave her in debt.'"

"Nathan," Nattie said patiently, "she may not have been entirely honest with you."

Silence.

"You weren't exactly honest with her, you know."

"What do you think I should do next?" he asked.

"If it were me, I'd follow her when she leaves work. It might be interesting to see if she lives like she's got no money."

"You think she's got more money than she let on?"

"I don't know for sure," confessed Nattie, "but if I was broke, I'd probably try to find a job somewhere instead of volunteering my time."

CHAPTER 22

Presly Holmes's Office

"'HAMBURGER ROW,'" ANNOUNCED KNOX as Nattie drove through the traffic light at Fort Henry Drive. "That's what Kevin calls this section of Kingsport, and that one's his favorite," she added when the Purple Cow came into view.

"How many stars?" asked Nattie. Kevin had a five-star scale for hamburgers. The meat, the bun, the condiments, the sides, and the atmosphere were all worth a point each.

"Four, I think," answered Knox. "They lose a point for just being a drive-through, but I think the shakes make up for that."

Nattie drove past Dunkin' Donuts and turned left to head downtown. "Downtown Kingsport is one of the best-kept secrets in the area," said Nattie. "I'll bet Kevin's never had a burger at JanMar. That'd be at least a four, too."

"Why do you say the downtown is a secret?"

"You'll see."

A few minutes later the two women were standing in front of P & J Antiques at the corner of Market and Broad. "This is the center of downtown," began Nattie. "You can go a couple of blocks in any direction, and you'll come to real interesting places. They've got art, crafts, coffee shops, restaurants."

"Look at the parking," noted Knox as she gazed down Broad Street, where the parking was diagonal and in the center of the street. "I've never seen parking like that."

"It's nice, isn't it?" said Nattie. "The streets all along here are twice as wide as they are in Bristol. It allows for a lot more parking."

"And there's still plenty of places to park."

"That's what I mean about this being a well-kept secret." She flipped her hand over. "I guess all the shoppers are at the mall." Shaking her head, "This could be a mini-Asheville with less hippies."

Nattie had a lot of history here in Kingsport. Standing on the corner of Market and Broad, much of it passed through her awareness like a slideshow. There was the now-defunct Freedom University, where she went for two years until she was told that having a beer in her room meant she didn't have enough integrity to keep her resident assistant job. It wasn't even her beer. But she never said anything. That was not her way.

She looked to her right toward the JanMar Grill. Her Freedom U. roommate, Jane, had a fondness for the burgers at JanMar because they buttered and toasted their buns on the grill.

Across the street was the Haggle House. Sunny Hill had a counter in there. She was in prison now, which was right, but it wasn't completely right.

Down Market Street was the Mustard Seed. Nathan had taken her there for lunch once. They had stood in front of the Suzanne Barrett Justis Gallery and watched the artist work on a tiger.

Then she looked to her left. It wasn't until she looked that way that she noticed she had been avoiding the view. That's where she had first met Trace Noble. He had an upstairs office about mid-block overlooking Broad Street.

"Where to?" asked Knox.

The question snapped Nattie back into the present. With a shake of her head she asked, "I'm sorry. I think I was taking a trip down memory lane there for a bit. How long was I gone?"

"Not long," answered Knox. "I couldn't tell if it was a pleasant trip or not."

Nattie looked full-faced at Knox. She was often surprised at how much Knox noticed, because she mostly looked like she didn't notice anything. "I couldn't tell either," she confessed, then she pointed to her left and added, "I think it's that way."

About mid-block Nattie found the address she was looking for and entered the building. She was thankful they were on the west side of Broad Street. When Kevin first gave her the address, she feared she might have to return to Trace Noble's old office. The thought of that psychopath chilled her. He tried to kill her—twice. He had come close both times. He was in prison again, and that was completely right.

Attorney Presly Holmes's office was on the second floor.

"Good morning," said a petite woman with reddish-brown hair and brown eyes. Standing in the middle of the reception area with a small watering can in her hands, she smiled at them as they entered. She was fair skinned, and her uniform was a dark blue pullover shirt, light brown vest, and designer blue jeans.

"Hi," said Nattie.

Knox smiled and nodded.

"Are y'all here to see Mr. Holmes?" the blonde asked as she sat down the watering can near a plant in the corner. "He's out of the office, but I can set up an appointment for you if you like." She walked to the opposite corner where a desk sat diagonally facing the large room. Once she was seated she took out an appointment book from the center drawer and opened it. Placing it on the desk she looked up and flashed another huge smile.

Nattie, who had followed her to her corner, looked down at the desk. "When will he be back?"

"He's on *another* golf trip," explained the woman. "He'll be back next week. What's this about?"

The name plaque on the desk read Kayleigh Buckner. On the wall behind her chair were numerous pictures of wolves. "Kayleigh—first, is it okay if I call you 'Kayleigh'?"

Kayleigh nodded yes.

"These pictures are amazing," said Nattie. "They're not prints, are they?"

"No. They're photographs."

"Did you take these pictures?"

"I did," beamed Kayleigh.

"How did you get such close-up shots of their faces? It's like you were in the pack."

Kayleigh snickered. "I kinda was. Do you know about the wolf habitat up on Bays Mountain?"

"I've never been there," said Nattie, "but I've heard about it. Were all these taken there?"

"Yeah. My husband, Mark, and I can't have kids, so we sorta adopted that wolf pack as ours. We're on the volunteer team to help with the pack."

"That's interesting," said Nattie. "It must be fun."

"Yeah, it is. In the summer they let small groups camp out next to the habitat. Wolves are mostly nocturnal, so it's a chance to see them more active. Mark and I serve as wolf guides five or six times every summer."

"Hey," said Nattie, "I heard that the wolves escaped once. Is that true?"

"December 4, 2009," answered Tracey immediately. "There was a blustery storm that night, and it blew over a tree in the habitat. Six wolves climbed up the tree and over the fence." With her hand she demonstrated the motioned of going up an incline and then over a fence. "All six of them came back within a few days."

"That's amazing," said Nattie. "And these pictures are amazing, too. I especially like the close-ups of their faces."

"It's the eyes," said Kayleigh.

Nattie found herself mesmerized by the close-up photo of a white wolf with golden highlights. It was the largest picture in the collage. The eyes were intense, but the wolf seemed to be smiling.

"That's Kawoni," said Kayleigh. "She's the one who escaped twice. She died shortly after that."

"She's beautiful," said Nattie.

"Yes."

"Well, Kayleigh," Nattie shifted her tone, handing the woman a business card, "my name is Nattie Moreland. I'm a PI from Bristol, and I'm here on behalf of Federation Fidelity Insurance Company."

Kayleigh studied the card and then slowly read it out loud, "Na-tash-a Mic-Mor-al-us." When she was done she looked up and smiled again. She asked none of the questions nor made any of the comments Nattie had come to expect when passing out her card. "How about next Tuesday morning?" asked Kayleigh.

"What time?"

"Is ten okay?"

Nattie nodded.

"And is the appointment for you or for Ms. McMorales?"

"There is no Ms. McMorales," explained Nattie. "That's just the name for the agency. I'm the detective."

"I see. Is this concerning the theft at his home?"

"It is," answered Nattie. "How did you know that?"

Kayleigh finished writing out an appointment card. As she handed it to Nattie she said, "You said you were representing Federation Fidelity, so I assumed it was about that robbery. Did they find some of the art?"

"I know some coins have turned up, but I don't know about any of the artwork," answered Nattie. "You sound like you know about the case. Were you working with Mr. Holmes at that time?"

"I was," Kayleigh told her. "I began working here on September 9, 1998."

"Nice memory," observed Nattie.

"I'm good at dates," blushed Kayleigh.

"What do you remember about the robbery?"

"I remember how devastated they were when it happened."

"Who?" asked Nattie.

"The Holmeses," responded Kayleigh in a tone that said the answer should have been obvious. "I think it did their marriage in."

"They're not together anymore?"

"No."

"Do you remember that date, too?"

"Certainly. I handle all the legal papers around here. They were divorced on May 15, 2010," said Kayleigh, shaking her head. "It's a shame. Their kids would have been beautiful."

"Anything else?"

"Like what?" asked Kayleigh.

"Anything from that time. Anything at all."

"I just remember the investigation afterward mostly. I still think it was that builder, but they couldn't prove it was him."

"Avery Heart?"

"That sounds right."

"Do you remember anything about that day? That night?"

"It was a normal day at the office. My husband, Mark, and I went to Gatlinburg right after work. We've got a cabin down there."

"How was the weather that day?" asked Nattie.

"The weather that day," repeated Kayleigh, looking out the window. She curled her lip and shook her head slowly back and forth, "I don't remember how the weather was then." Looking back at Nattie she said, "I don't remember that detail. That was four or five years ago, wasn't it?"

"Did Mr. Holmes receive copies of the police reports?"

"No, I don't believe so."

"As the claimant, he may have gotten reports from the insurance company," said Nattie. "Do you remember if that happened?"

Without taking her eyes off Nattie, Kayleigh tipped her head to the right, "It did."

Nattie softened her voice. "You read that report, didn't you?"

Kayleigh squinted as her whole face went taut as she pulled in her right eyebrow. "I didn't do anything wrong. I open and screen all of Mr. Holmes's mail."

"Of course," said Nattie softly. "That wasn't a confidential document, and even if it was, Mr. Holmes would have had the right to share it with whomever he chose."

Kayleigh still looked suspiciously at Nattie. "What is it that you want, Miss Morales?"

"I think the Federation Fidelity report said there were tire tracks from a truck in the mud outside the room that was broken into, but I'm not sure I'm remembering right. I was hoping you might remember."

Kayleigh shook her head no.

"It's just that when I try to reconstruct the robbery, I have to picture enough time to break through the wall of a house and then to load a small truck with a significant art collection, knowing that the thieves would have to be careful with the art to maintain its value. Do you have a guess on how long that would take?"

Kayleigh shrugged. "Hours, I guess." She tugged her eyebrow again. "Why?"

"I'm not sure," said Nattie. "I'm just trying to get it pictured in my mind. It's curious to me that someone could dig a hole through the wall of a house and then park a small truck on the lawn next to it for hours and not be noticed by any of the neighbors." Pointing at Kayleigh, Nattie continued, "You've been to that house, right?"

Kayleigh pulled her head back slightly. "Yes," she answered tentatively.

"Well, is it so isolated that a neighbor wouldn't notice something like that?"

"It's not really in a neighborhood," explained Kayleigh. "There are houses on either side of it, but there's a lot of trees between them, too."

"So is it plausible that a neighbor would not have noticed all that commotion?"

"Yeah. Especially if it was raining, like you said."

"But you don't remember if it was raining."

"I'll bet you could Google it," suggested Knox, who had been looking more closely at the wolf photos behind Kayleigh's desk. "Cool pictures. Did you take these?"

"Thank you," said Kayleigh. "I did."

"Do you think Mr. Holmes would meet me at his house next Tuesday instead of meeting here at his office?" asked Nattie.

"If you mean the house in the woods, no. He doesn't live there anymore. Ginger got that house in the divorce."

"Of course," said Nattie. "Do you think Mrs. Holmes would meet with me there?"

"You'd have to ask her."

Nattie handed the appointment card back to Kayleigh. "Would you mind putting her phone number on the back of the card, please?"

Kayleigh took the card and wrote down Ginger Holmes's phone number.

CHAPTER 23

The Holmes's Home

THE HOLMES'S HOME WASN'T HOMEY AT ALL. It was an isolated showpiece. The setting: a long winding driveway that wound up the side of a knob. A knob is what the people of Indiana would have called a hill. Except for the top and where the driveway had been cut, the knob was covered in well-established trees. There were log cabins on either side of it, but both were so low and so distant that neither could be seen from the top, nor could anyone at the cabins see the top. The setting called for a large log cabin or hunting-lodge type of home instead of the ornate Mediterranean estate that it held.

Nattie was a bit surprised when Ginger Holmes answered the door herself.

"Are you the private investigator?" she asked. She looked to be in her forties with unnaturally light blonde hair done in a hairstyle that would have fit on the set of *Mad Men.* She wore a pale blue housedress with a string of small pearls around her neck. She would have been pretty if her foundation makeup had not been so thick.

"I am. Thank you for seeing us," said Nattie. "This is Knox . . . ," began Nattie, but she wasn't sure whether to use Knox's real last name, Farmer, or her stage name, DeVilla.

"Berry Farm," suggested Ginger.

"I should use that sometime," smiled Knox. "Actually my name is Candace Farmer. Knox DeVilla is my stage name." Smiling at Nattie, "My friends call me Knox."

"Come in," said Ginger, swinging the door all the way open.

"We'll sit in the sunroom," she told them once they were both in the foyer. She led them through a formal living room, which was decorated more for a hunting lodge than as the 1950s showpiece Nattie expected after seeing the outside. The high ceiling with exposed beams of timber crowned the airy room. The furniture was wooden mission style with light brown accents.

The art on the walls was an eclectic assortment of prints of classic pieces. Nattie recognized *The Scream* by Munch. She stopped in front of it and said, "This is an unusual piece for a living room."

"I know," said Ginger. "It reminds me of a trip to Oslo, though."

"Wow," said Knox from behind them. "That *is* interesting."

"It's called *Nightmare*," said Ginger.

The comment made Nattie flinch. She looked at Ginger expecting a smile or some other indication that she was joking. She saw none.

Knox held up her cell phone. "Do you mind if I take a picture? My boyfriend would think this was cool."

"Not at all," said Ginger.

Knox took two pictures. "Thanks," she said as she turned toward the stone fireplace. "This is pretty cool, too."

Knox was looking at a large painting of Bob Barker that hung above the fireplace mantle.

Knox raised her camera but was immediately admonished.

"I'd rather you not take any pictures of that," said Ginger immediately. In a snooty voice she added, "It's an original. Serious art collectors are kind of finicky about having their originals photographed. It degrades the oils."

"Oh, I'm sorry," said Knox. "I didn't know."

Serious art collector? thought Nattie. *Incredible. You thought* The Scream *was called "Nightmare," and you own it.*

"That's quite all right," said Ginger in a nasally patronizing tone. "You didn't know. Please follow me."

She led them to another room just off the living room. The sunroom was very cozy, with upholstered wicker furniture and plenty of plants. It was two steps lower than the living room and surrounded on three sides by glass walls.

"I have just about a half hour before I need to leave for a luncheon. One of my girlfriends is turning forty and," striking a fashion-magazine pose with her left hand on her left hip and sweeping her right hand down across her body, "that's why I'm dressed like June Cleaver. It's a *Leave It to Beaver* theme."

"That sounds fun," said Nattie. "We won't keep you long. As I told you on the phone, I'm Nattie Moreland, and I'm here representing the Federation Fidelity Insurance Company. As you know, they made a four-million-dollar payout on an art collection, but none of the art has reemerged."

"Is that unusual?" asked Ginger.

"A single rare piece of stolen art can get in the hands of a collector who keeps it as a treasure, but a collection this size was more likely taken for the money. So, it is unusual that none of it has begun showing up at auction houses or with art dealers."

Ginger nodded.

"More recently some of the gold coins have shown up on Bays Mountain."

"Is that what brought you to my door?"

"Yes," said Nattie.

"How can I help?" Ginger asked. To Knox she added, "If it will help you nail my ex, I'll help in any way I can."

"You think it was Mr. Holmes?" asked Nattie.

"I do," she said. "I've said that all along."

"What motive would he have to steal what he already owns?"

"He didn't own it. The art collection was mine. It was mine before we got married."

"So it wasn't marital property, but still it was in his possession."

"It wasn't going to be for long. I was divorcing him. If we had divorced, that art collection would have stayed with me."

Motive, thought Nattie. Presly Holmes had been a suspect before on the basis of opportunity. That he had motive as well was new. "I believe from the reports that I read that he had a fairly convincing alibi on the night of the robbery."

"He had an alibi for that night, but I had been gone for several days prior to that. I was in Europe with my mother. Presly was here all by himself for several days before the supposed break-in."

"Can you prove that?"

"Can I prove I was in Europe?" repeated Ginger. "I'm sure there are records of the flight and the hotels. I know we flew out of Tri-Cites on that Monday and had a layover in Charlotte, and then we were on an overnight British Airways flight that went directly to Heathrow. If you need the hotel we stayed in, I can probably get that from my mother."

"I think the flight info will do it, but I'll let you know if I need more." Standing up, Nattie said, "You've been quite helpful, thank you. We'll let you go to your *Leave It to Beaver* lunch."

Ginger walked them to the door. As they left she said, "Please let me know if there's anything else I can do to help. Nothing would give me more pleasure."

●　●　●

The thought that she may have neglected Knox for most of the morning dawned on Nattie as soon as she started the car. She wanted to say something but decided to wait until they were off the winding driveway. The trip down went a bit faster than it had driving up.

"So," began Nattie, "what do you think of Mrs. Holmes?"

"She's either guilty, or she's still really pissed off at her husband."

Nattie grinned. "I'd say it's a safe bet she's still pissed at him, and she definitely gave us a motive for him, but what makes you think she might be guilty?"

"I'm not saying I think she's guilty. I mean, she knew she was gonna push him at you even before we got there."

"Is that a hunch, or did you notice something?"

"When I told her Knox is my stage name, she didn't ask what I did." Knox tipped her head sideways and added, "Most people automatically ask if I'm an actor when I tell them it's a stage name. I figured she was already focused on something else."

"Very nice observation," said Nattie. "Very nice."

Knox smiled, "Watching you work was fun. I'm glad you asked me to come."

"Me, too."

CHAPTER 24

Saturday Powwow
at Price's Store

HIRAM SAT AT ONE END OF THE TABLE. Nattie sat at the other. Kevin and Knox sat together with their backs to the drink cooler while Nathan sat facing them. They had all already gone through the breakfast buffet line and given their egg order to Mark Price, owner and grill man.

When the eggs were brought to the table, Nattie asked, "Are we getting pumpkin pancakes, too?"

"Not this time of year, honey," said Mark from behind the counter.

Nattie had to turn all the way around in her seat to face Mark.

"We only do that when the pumpkin is fresh. Maybe September. For sure by October," he told her. "I'm so glad you like them."

After they were all done eating breakfast, the conversation turned toward business. Hiram, the retired PI who had mentored Nattie when the agency was his, presided over the powwow. It wasn't that he had started the powwow sessions back when he was in charge, because he hadn't. These powwow sessions were Nattie's idea. It was her version of brainstorming. She reckoned that with cases that were more complicated, it was good to meet regularly to make sure everyone knew what everyone else was doing. A fresh set of eyes meant a fresh perspective, and Hiram taking the lead meant getting somewhere different than where Nattie would have gone.

"Do you want to start us off?" Hiram asked Nattie.

"Sure," she said. "Knox and I went over to Kingsport to call on the Holmeses. They owned the home that was burglarized. First we went to Presly Holmes's law office. He wasn't in, but we've got an appointment with him next week."

"Any impressions?" asked Hiram.

Nattie nodded at Knox.

"We didn't meet him, but his office is fairly unimpressive. It's just him and his legal secretary."

"Did you think she was a legal secretary?" asked Nattie. "I thought she was pretty loose-lipped and unprofessional."

"You're right," agreed Knox. "But she sure liked wolves."

"So he doesn't look like a millionaire lawyer," offered Nathan.

Nattie looked at Knox and nodded.

"If he's the thief, he didn't spend the money on his office," observed Knox. "That doesn't mean he doesn't have it," she added. "On the other hand, he's got enough money to take a bunch of golf trips."

"How do you know that?" asked Hiram.

"When Nattie asked if he was in, his secretary said, 'He's on *another* golf trip.' It seemed like it happened more than she approved of. Besides, his ex-wife sure thinks it's him."

"That was our second stop," explained Nattie. "Knox is right; his ex was very quick to point a finger at him. Maybe too quick."

"Let's slow down," said Hiram, holding his hands out. "Have we discussed the lawyer enough? We don't want to move on to the wife until we finish with the husband."

Nattie waited for Knox to answer first, but Knox kept quiet. "Presly Holmes is still a solid suspect in my mind. We always knew he had means and opportunity, but according to his ex-wife, he had plenty of motive, too."

"What's the motive?" asked Nathan.

Nattie swept her hand, palm up, toward Knox.

Knox sat up straighter, moving her chair at bit closer to the table. "That stolen art—that was Mrs. Holmes's before she got married, so it would have been all hers when they got divorced. He's a lawyer, so he would have known that."

"So, even though it was all hers from before, he got half the insurance money because the policy came after they were married," said Nathan with a frown. "Does that sound right?"

"Not to me," said Hiram.

"We can check that out with Lionel," said Nattie, "but I'm thinking that it all depends on how the insurance papers were written."

Kevin cleared his throat, drawing all the attention his way. "I don't have the papers here in front of me, but if I remember correctly, I think the entire insurance payout was to Mr. Holmes, not Mr. and Mrs. Holmes."

A silence followed the observation.

"So he is a crook," chortled Nathan finally.

"But he's not necessarily our crook," added Nattie.

Nathan lifted his right-hand index finger up. "Not *necessarily.*"

"Mr. Holmes is definitely a prime suspect," declared Hiram. "Are we ready to move to the wife?"

"Just a minute," said Nattie. She asked Kevin, "What else have you got on Holmes?"

"There's not really much to tell about him," began Kevin. "He's from Idaho. He went to college in Idaho on a golf scholarship. He went to law school at UT. That's where he met Ginger Tomlinson." Kevin quickly looked around the table before adding, "She got married so she wouldn't be 'Ginger Tea' anymore."

No one said, "A pun is the lowest form of humor," but no one needed to either. He got a pity smile from Knox.

Enjoy it while you can, bro, 'cause she won't find that cute for long, Nattie told him in her head.

Kevin chuckled, unfazed by doing so alone. "It took him three tries to pass the bar exam. After that he worked for three different firms in the span of two years before getting married and starting his own practice in Kingsport. I couldn't find out why he left those other firms, but he probably came to Kingsport to be near his wife's family. His father-in-law, Ben Tomlinson, is the president of a bank and owns property all over the Tri-Cities. Mr. Holmes has expensive taste; he likes sports cars, he takes a lot of trips to play golf, and he goes to a lot of big sporting events."

"Like what?" asked Nathan.

"Super Bowl, Final Four, Rose Bowl, and he's got a skybox at Bristol Motor Speedway."

"I take it his law practice does not support that lifestyle," suggested Hiram.

"Not even close," said Kevin, "but he married money, and that's been his lifestyle since then."

"And he got the whole four-and-a-half-million dollar payout from the insurance claim," interjected Nattie. "So the divorce didn't end the gravy train."

"That would sure be motive to point a finger at him," noted Hiram.

"She's got money," said Nattie. "I think she may have been in such a hurry to rid herself of him that she didn't bother fighting for the insurance money."

"Let's slow down a little," said Hiram. "Was their divorce before or after the burglary?"

"After. Why?" asked Nattie.

"According to you, he wrote that insurance policy so that he'd get all the money, but that would only work if the divorce comes after the burglary."

"True," said Nattie with a frown. "That means that coldhearted sociopath was probably planning the divorce for a while."

"It means he may have planned the burglary, too," offered Kevin.

"Maybe he did," admitted Nathan. "But maybe all he did was to hire the right contractor to make sure that safe room was vulnerable."

"Like baiting a trap," said Hiram.

"That poor woman," sighed Knox. "I thought she was a snot, but I almost feel sorry for her. She probably thought her marriage was okay while that—what did you call him, Nattie?"

"Sociopath."

Knox nodded toward Nattie before continuing, "She probably thought her life was going along fine while that social-patio was plotting all this."

"Maybe not," said Kevin. "I checked out the happy couple in *VIPSeen* magazine. They were pictured together at four or five events every year until 2007. After that there are fewer pictures, and none with them together."

"So something was amiss for a few years before their divorce," observed Nattie.

"I still feel sorry for her," said Knox.

"But how do you like her as a suspect?" asked Hiram.

"She certainly had opportunity and probably had the means, but money wouldn't have been the motive," said Nattie. "I wouldn't cross her off the list just yet, but I don't think we should spend much time pursuing her." She looked toward Kevin and asked, "Could you verify her alibi?"

"The hotel she said she stayed in has changed ownership since then, but she and her mother were definitely on a flight to London two days before the burglary and they didn't return until December 15."

"What about her background, Kevin?" asked Hiram.

"I didn't really look at her. She grew up in Kingsport, and I already told you about her father," answered Kevin apologetically. To Nattie he said, "I can look more closely at her if you want."

Nattie nodded. "You might as well, but consider it a low priority."

"Yeah," agreed Nathan, "we've got bigger fish here."

All heads turned to Nathan.

"Okay, Nate," said Hiram, sitting back in his chair. "What have you got?"

Nathan sat back, too. He casually crossed his legs and cleared his throat.

He's doing the professor, Nattie told herself.

"I was in Alexandria this week following up on the contractor," explained Nathan. "As you know, he was the prime suspect in the investigation four years ago, but his alibi was solid—so he didn't do the actual robbery, but he could have planned it. He had firsthand knowledge of how vulnerable that safe room was, so he could have had a confederate."

"What did you find out?" asked Hiram.

"I connected with his wife, Shannon. He's doing a two-year stint in Jersey for tax evasion. Shannon moved to Alexandria after he lost all their money and filed bankruptcy."

"Actually," said Kevin, "that's not right."

"What do you mean?" snapped Nathan, jutting his chin across the table at Kevin. "I'm repeating *exactly* what she told me."

Another hushed silence washed over the table. Kevin immediately raised both palms and leaned back.

Hiram broke the tension. "Alexandria *is* an odd place to move to if you're out of money."

Nathan settled back in his chair. "Her son is a historian at Mount Vernon. She moved there to be close to him." Nathan pointed at Nattie. "I followed her like you told me. She does live in an expensive gated subdivision, so she's not living like she's broke."

"So that moves him up on the suspect list," said Hiram.

"You'd think so," said Nathan quickly, "but a new suspect has arisen."

Again, Hiram held his palms out. "Let's finish with the contractor before we move on to someone else."

Nathan nodded. "I'll concede that Shannon Heart's living arrangements have to be explained, but something new has happened that lessens how good her husband looks as a suspect." He paused, looking from face to face, before saying, "Some of the coins have shown up."

"You've already shared that," said Nattie. "Do you have more info now?"

"It was a little more than a month ago. And it was on Bays Mountain."

"Wait a minute," said Hiram. "Why does that have any bearing on the contractor's viability as a suspect?"

"Because," said Nathan, tapping the table with his index finger, "Avery Heart is still in prison *and* there's no connection between him and Bays Mountain. But there is someone else who does have a connection." Nathan bowed his head and spread his hands as if inviting the question he had orchestrated.

"That's still not right," said Kevin cautiously.

Noisily inhaling through clenched teeth, Nathan snarled, *"What?"*

The reactions to Nathan's tone varied around the table. Kevin flinched. Hiram and Nattie both looked at Nathan with raised eyebrows. Knox glared.

"Nathan," said Nattie gently, "Kevin didn't mean to insult you."

"Calling me a liar," stated Nathan. "That's not insulting?"

"He said your information was not right," said Hiram in a lower voice. "He did not call you a liar."

"Okay, little brother, what wasn't right?" Nathan said the words "little brother" in a singsongy whine.

"Avery Heart was released from prison two months ago," stated Kevin sheepishly as he made eye contact with everyone but Nathan.

"Where is he now?" asked Hiram.

"I don't know," answered Kevin. "He's fallen off the grid."

Yet another awkward silence followed.

"Nathan, please explain the deal with the coins on Bays Mountain again for Hiram," Nattie said, finally breaking the tension.

"I got this from Federation Fidelity, so it's fresh, but some gold coins like the ones that were stolen from the Holmeses turned up near a shelter on Bays Mountain. There aren't serial numbers on coins, but still these are pretty distinctive coins, so it's quite a coincidence."

"What makes them distinctive?" asked Nattie.

"They aren't old," explained Nathan, "but they are all one-ounce gold pieces. Each one has a spouse of a president on it. I don't remember all three, but I'm pretty sure one was Martha Washington."

"What does it mean that coins 'turned up'?" asked Hiram.

Nathan glared at his uncle.

"Were they laying around on the ground? Or were they in a hole or under a board?"

"It was three coins, and they were found by one of the staff early in the morning," answered Nathan defensively. "I don't know where they were found, but they also found a hole near a new shelter. The hole had been dug up overnight and then filled back in." He tipped his head forward once.

"Are you saying that someone may have buried those coins there before and then a month ago dug them back up?" suggested Nattie.

"And on the way from the hole dropped three of them," added Hiram.

"That's what I thought," said Nathan curtly.

"So, Avery Heart could have buried them there before leaving Kingsport and then dug them up after getting released," said Nattie.

"The timing for that works," added Kevin.

"Yes," agreed Knox.

"But," said Nathan, a little calmer this time, "there's no connection between Avery and that shelter, but there is a connection to another one of the original suspects."

"Which one?" asked Nattie.

Nathan took a small Moleskin notebook from his back pocket and opened it. "The Kingsport building inspector. He was the inspector who oversaw that addition to the Holmes's home. As you say, Avery Heart had firsthand knowledge of the safe room's vulnerability, but so did Mr. Stout. *And* he was the inspector for that shelter on Bays Mountain, which, by the way, was being constructed at the same time as the robbery."

"What do we know about this . . . what was his name again?" asked Nattie.

"Alexander Sebastian Stout," read Nathan.

"What do we know about him?" Nattie repeated.

"I can check him out," said Kevin. "'Alexander Sebastian Stout.' He sounds like an ass to me."

As if it was the first time he had used the joke, Kevin grinned. He stopped grinning when he looked at Knox, who was shaking her head no.

Good for you, thought Nattie.

"Federation is pushing Kingsport toward this guy," said Nathan. "So if he's our crook, they're already ahead of us."

Nattie studied his face. "What are you suggesting we do differently?"

"He should be at the top of our suspect list," stated Nathan.

"Meaning that's where we put our time and effort?" asked Nattie.

"Of course. He's as good a candidate as any of them, but we're behind Kingsport in pursuing him."

Nattie looked away from Nathan. "Can we all agree that we have three good candidates right now?"

Everyone but Knox nodded yes.

"Knox," said Nattie firmly.

Knox shook her head like she was waking up. "I'm sorry."

"Do you agree that we have three good suspects?"

"Sure," said Knox with a shrug.

"We've opened investigations on Heart and Holmes already, and I think I should stay with Holmes for a while longer. But does anyone agree with Nathan shifting his investigation from Heart to Stout?"

Nathan made a show of loudly inhaling and exhaling. "I'm paying my own expenses here, so I'm going to be shifting with or without anyone's agreement."

"I see," said Nattie.

"Is that a problem?" he asked.

"The decision isn't a problem at all, and if you'd let us talk about it we may have even agreed with you, but your attitude *is* a problem," asserted Nattie.

A surprised look crossed Nathan's face.

"You about bit Kevin's head off because he corrected you, which was his job. You went to see Shannon, and he went to cyberspace; you were *supposed* to come back with different information. This is either a team effort or it isn't. And if it's a team, we all bring different things to the table, *and* it works best if we appreciate each others' contributions."

The silence at the table was pungent. Nathan's lips were pressed together, and his breathing was shallow. He looked like he was ready to explode. "What do you want me to do?"

"I think it'd be nice if you were receptive to any input we might have about the merits of the Heart versus Stout investigations," answered Nattie.

"What have you got?" he asked with a scan of the table.

Come on, thought Nattie. *Someone speak.*

Knox cleared her throat. "I don't know which one should be focused on, and I don't know why they can't be given equal time, but I do know what should happen next." She locked her eyes on Nathan.

Nathan stared across the table at Knox. "What?" he snarled.

"You owe Kevin an apology."

Nathan slowly shifted his glare from Knox to Kevin. Kevin held his gaze.

Screwing his face into an obviously fake and exaggerated smile, Nathan mimicked a little girl's voice, "Sorry, Kevin."

The table was speechless. Kevin and Knox looked at Nathan in shocked disbelief. Nattie and Hiram looked at each other.

Nathan stood up with a jerk and announced, "I got the check." Then he turned and walked away without looking back. Not until he was out the front door did anyone speak.

"What was that?" asked Kevin.

Nattie and Hiram looked at each other again. Nattie shrugged slightly. Hiram responded with a nod.

"I've never seen him so surly like that, but Nathan's been diagnosed as bipolar and that could be it," said Nattie.

"I've seen him blow up over something little like that," said Kevin.

"When?" asked Nattie.

"It was a couple of years ago. We were driving down the parkway and pulled into a gas station to get coffee. We didn't need gas, but he had to park next to a pump anyway because someone had parked sideways across all the parking places in front." Kevin grinned at the memory. "I thought he was gonna get us killed. The guy wasn't that big, but he was built." Kevin mimed a muscle-bound guy. "Nathan asked him if he thought four parking places was enough."

"What happened?" asked Hiram.

"The guy said he was sorry and left. But I'm telling you, Nathan was ready to go. And that guy would have had no trouble whupping our butts."

"Is that part of bipolar?" asked Knox.

"I think it can be, but anger isn't usual for Nathan. With him it's more like he gets impulsive or grandiose," said Nattie.

"And self-medicating," added Hiram. "That's what the doctor told us."

"All I know is that he was rude, and then he was rude again when he apologized," stated Knox.

"I know," Nattie sighed. "You're right. I'll talk to him." Nathan brought out the strongest and most unstable feelings in her. She had gone from furious at him to protective pity in the time it took him to walk out the door.

She sighed again and turned back to the table. "That's probably enough fun for one day. Does anyone have any last comments?"

Knox raised her hand. "If it was the contractor who dug up those coins on Bays Mountain, then the timing makes sense, but if it was the building inspector, then why dig it up now?"

Why now, indeed? thought Nattie.

CHAPTER 25

Saturday Breakfast [Jack]

"OKAY," ALICE SAID, "WHERE ARE YOU?"

I was staring out the window at nothing in the Perkins parking lot. "What do you mean?"

She gave me one of those raised-eyebrow, I-know-you-know-I-know looks. "You sure weren't here. Where were you?"

"Nowhere in particular," I said.

"Just not here," she huffed.

"I'm sorry," I apologized. "I guess I'm not very good company."

"Nice try, sport. Something's eating at you, and I want to know what it is." She tapped the table firmly.

"Do you think you deserve everything that goes through my head?"

She frowned. "First of all, I don't know if we're talking about good stuff in your head or bad stuff in your head, so I have no idea what I deserve. But I do know I *deserve* your presence here at breakfast. You committed it to me, and now you're giving it to something else. I want to know what. Come on, something's bothering you. Don't make me wrestle it out of you."

"Is that a threat?"

She laughed. "It is if you're scared." She eyed me, "Somehow I don't think you're scared."

"They're bringing Hout back," I blurted.

"Doug," she clarified.

"Yeah."

"Why?"

"I met with the city manager yesterday morning, and he said they were bringing Doug back to 'take the pressure off me.'"

She put her hand on mine. "Has there been a problem?"

"No. Not at all," he said. "It's just until the dust settles from this investigation."

"And that bothers you?"

Does that bother me? Having someone who could replace me coming in to "help"—why would that bother me? "Yeah, that bothers me."

"Doug Hout is your friend," she reminded me.

"I know."

"He's retired. He's not after your job. Franny would never move back here from Arizona."

"Have you forgotten? Franny died in December." Franny was Doug's wife. They moved to Arizona because of her asthma. She had a massive heart attack in December. Doug didn't let anyone know, though, until mid-January. He said he didn't want to disturb anyone's Christmas.

A pained look crossed Alice's face as she remembered. It bothered her that she had forgotten.

"But you're right. Doug is my friend. He's not after my job." I rubbed the back of her hand as it rested on top of mine. "But that doesn't mean my job is safe."

That's when Carol came to the table with our breakfast. We had both ordered our usual. Alice got a waffle. I had a country Benedict with sausage and sawmill gravy. We went out for breakfast at least once a month. Part of the ritual was to read the passage of the Bible we would be studying in Sunday school the next day, but we usually did that before our breakfast came.

When Carol took our dishes, Alice asked for more coffee, which she almost never did. When we ate breakfast at Perkins on Saturday morning, she'd always have a Walmart-Target list, and she'd want to get to those places before they got too busy. Today she asked for more coffee.

"Let's read," she told me as she took her too-small-for-me-to-read Bible from her purse.

"Genesis thirty-two, verses twenty-two to twenty-nine," she began. Our class was working its way through Genesis. The passage of the day was Jacob wrestling with the angel all night.

"Do you think Jacob knew it was an angel he was wrestling?" asked Alice as soon as she was done reading.

"Not until they were done and the angel popped his hip," I told her. I always figured that was the angel's way of telling him, "I could have whupped you anytime I wanted."

"So Jacob didn't know it was God at work while he was struggling through it," she said nonchalantly.

She's deliberately not looking at me. I know what she's up to. "Is that really the passage for class?"

"Of course," she said, but she still didn't look at me.

"So you think I'm worrying for nothing."

Now she looked at me.

"Do you think I'm wrestling with an angel?"

"I don't know about an angel, but I don't believe we'll know what God is doing in this until we get to the next day." She smiled and corrected herself—"until the dust settles."

She was right, and I knew it. It even made me feel a little better, but that didn't keep me from wanting this night to be over.

"Remind me not to wrestle with you," I told her.

CHAPTER 26

Sunday Lunch:
Nattie Meets Jack

NATTIE EXHALED LOUDLY AS THE O'BRIEN HOUSE came into view.

"What?" asked Kevin.

"Nothing," she told him. She hadn't meant to be so obvious, but she was relieved to see a midnight-blue Ram pickup in her parents' driveway. That meant someone was joining them for Sunday lunch, which also meant a reprieve from her mother's questions. "What else was so important that you missed church? Nice of you to finally get here! What's new with you and Nathan? When will you get a respectable job?" Innocent questions asked by anyone else were handled with ease, but the same questions coming from Ingrid inevitably triggered a mother–junior high daughter reaction from Nattie. To make it worse, Ingrid almost never asked innocent questions.

"Did Trevor get a new truck?" asked Kevin as they parked on the street in front of the house.

"I don't know whose truck that is. Mom said Sam and her clan were at a camp in North Carolina this weekend."

"So who's the mystery guest?"

Natalie shrugged, "Probably someone from their church."

Kevin leaned toward her, speaking softly, "It could be someone Mom wants to fix you up with."

Nattie opened the storm door and nodded for Kevin to go first. "You better be careful, sport. It could be the men in the white coats."

Kevin just smiled and opened the front door. "We're here," he announced before stepping back and ushering Nattie through first.

They heard laughter coming from the dining room as they entered. *That's a good sign,* thought Nattie.

"Sorry we're late," said Nattie as she entered the dining room.

"You're not late," said Lionel from his usual spot at the head of the table.

To Lionel's left, on the side of the table where Nattie and Kevin usually sat, was a couple who must have been the owners of the truck in the driveway. They were close in age to Ingrid, late fifties or so. The woman smiled warmly at them when they entered. She had clear blue eyes, a pretty face, but more than anything else she looked . . . nice. Her husband, who had stood up as Nattie entered, looked as uncomfortable as his wife looked at ease. He was wide—big shoulders, big hands, and an even bigger middle. He looked like an athlete who hadn't been athletic for a long time.

"This is Jack and Alice," announced Ingrid. "And that's Natalie and Kevin, two of our three kids."

Nattie smiled. "Good to meet you. Please sit."

"Hey," said Kevin as he circled the table to shake hands with Jack, "you must be the funny one."

Jack looked confused.

"We heard you guys laughing when we came in," explained Nattie.

"Yeah," agreed Kevin, flipping his thumb back and forth between Ingrid and Lionel. "And I didn't think it was these two."

"I resent that," grinned Lionel. "I say funny things all the time."

Nattie, Ingrid, and Kevin all turned toward him.

"Okay, not *all* the time."

"Kevin's our comedian," said Ingrid. Jack and Alice smiled at him.

"That's me," smiled Kevin, "the family clown."

"Not 'clown,'" scolded Ingrid. "'Wit.'" To Jack and Alice she explained, "He especially likes to throw one-liners at Lionel when we discuss the Bible." To Kevin she said, "But you missed it today, sweetheart. We were discussing the sermon, and Jack got off a one-liner you'd have really appreciated."

All the attention turned to Jack.

"How about a replay?" requested Kevin as he circled the table again to take a seat next to Lionel and across from Alice. Nattie took the seat across from Jack.

Jack settled back in his seat. "I don't remember," he said unconvincingly.

"I do," announced Ingrid. "Lionel was quoting from the Sermon on the Mount, and when he said, 'Don't worry about what you wear or what you eat,' Jack said—"

"'Not worrying about what I eat is why I have to worry about what I wear,'" interrupted Lionel.

The two couples laughed heartily. That was the way it was with the retelling of a funny moment. For those who experienced it the first time around, their enjoyment was in the remembering. For those who are being told about it, their enjoyment is in watching the others, which can be just as entertaining.

Kevin managed a chuckle. "Good one," he said earnestly.

Jack, whose head was down slightly, looked up as Kevin complimented him, but he didn't look at Kevin. He looked directly at Nattie and then quickly looked away.

Whoa, said Nattie to herself, *what was that?* That he came up looking at her instead of Kevin unnerved her. His looking away when he caught her watching him made it worse. *Eeeeew.* There was a queasy feeling that seemed to start in her belly and spread up to her head. She shook her head to make it go away. *The guy's just embarrassed and on the spot,* she told herself. *He's harmless. His wife is sitting right here next to him.*

"Thank you," he said to Kevin.

"So," said Kevin, "how did you all meet?"

"We met in high school," answered Alice.

Jack leaned toward his wife and whispered, "I think he means how did we meet Lionel and Ingrid."

Alice shrunk a little.

"That's okay," said Kevin. "I just didn't know I wanted to hear how you two met."

Nattie watched as Alice glanced sheepishly at Jack. *Is she asking for permission to talk?* wondered Nattie.

"I was just a sophomore, and Jack was a senior. We had never had a class together or even spoken. I didn't know that he lived down the street from us until one day after football season he rode home on my bus. Jack sat all the way in the back by himself. In fact, I didn't notice he was there until he moved."

Out of the corner of her eye Nattie saw Jack roll his eyes. *Is this guy a jerk or what?*

"There was this boy—I didn't really know much about him, but he was kinda effeminate, and every day these other boys would sit behind him and make fun of him. It was awful. He'd just sit there and look out the window as if he couldn't hear them, but he couldn't have not heard them."

"I hate that," said Ingrid. "Kids can be so cruel."

"So, did you beat the hell out of them?" Kevin asked Jack.

The question drew a surprised look from Jack. His mouth was opened slightly, but he didn't say anything.

The question drew a reaction from Ingrid, too, but it was not surprise. Her glare said plenty. Kevin didn't notice.

"No," answered Alice. "What he did was even better. He walked up the aisle real slow, the way John Wayne would walk into a saloon. Everyone noticed him coming." She giggled. "We didn't know what he was going to do. Trudy, the girl I was sitting with, told me later she thought he was going to join in on the bullying, but that thought never entered my mind. I knew he wasn't that kind of guy just looking at him."

With that, everyone looked at Jack, who responded with a shrug and a tip of his head at Alice.

"What did he do?" asked Ingrid.

Alice smiled softly. "He asked that boy if he could sit down. He never even looked at those bullies. He just sat there talking to that boy."

"His name was Daniel," said Jack.

"No one had ever talked to Daniel on that bus before, but we could tell they were really talking about something."

"And the bullies?" asked Kevin.

Alice sat back and separated her hands, palms down, like she was calling the runner safe at home. "Not a peep," she announced. "Not just the rest of that day, but ever."

"A hero," said Lionel, lifting his iced tea. "Well played. Well played, indeed."

"I agree," said Kevin, lifting his iced tea in salute, "but this story is incomplete."

"Kevin," scolded Ingrid.

He looked down the table at his mother this time. "This was billed as a story of how they met." He turned to Alice and tipped his glass toward her. "It is a great story so far, but we want the rest. How did you meet?"

"We were the last two off the bus," said Jack.

"That's the short version," said Alice.

Jack rolled his eyes again.

What's with this guy? wondered Nattie once more. She had decided she liked Alice very much, but hero or not, Nattie had very little tolerance for Jack's treatment of his wife.

"Jack stayed with that boy, I mean Daniel, all the way. One of the bullies got off first, then Daniel, and then the other bully. After that Jack just sat there looking out the window until we got to the last stop, which was Trudy's stop. When she and I walked up the aisle, she asked him if he lived there. He said, 'No,' and that he was going back to the garage, but the bus driver said he had to get off there because it was the last stop."

"Did you let your stop go by?" asked Ingrid.

"He did," answered Alice. "He missed his stop so he could stay with Daniel."

Jack pointed at her with his thumb. "So did she."

"Not exactly," explained Alice. "I stayed to watch him." She pointed back at Jack. "And besides, I knew Trudy would give me a ride home."

"Trudy gave you both a ride home," guessed Kevin.

"Trudy was my best friend," smiled Alice. "She let me use her mother's car. We went to McDonald's."

CHAPTER 27

Sunday Lunch [Jack]

WE'RE DUE AT THE O'BRIENS' AT TWELVE-THIRTY, so of course I was still in the driveway waiting for Alice at twelve-twenty. We had already been to the early service at church and to our Sunday school class, so I wasn't sure what she needed to do to be ready for lunch. There was a time when I would wait patiently in the driveway tapping my horn periodically, but she threatened to shave my head while I slept the next time I did that, so waiting patiently without tapping the horn is what I do now.

We generally make decisions together very well. There are lots of things she cares about and I don't, so she decides all of those. And there are things I care about and she doesn't, so I decide those. When we both care about something, we can talk it out and come to a decision that works best. Then there is the unique decision about arriving somewhere on time. We've never come to an agreement about arriving anywhere on time, which means it is an undecided issue every time we go somewhere. When other marital issues are undecided, it might work out just by chance that each of us gets our way some of the time. But when one spouse wants to be early and the other late, the one who wants to be late will win every time.

Despite what I sound like, I have made peace with this phenomenon. I reckon it this way: If I knew then what I know now, would I still have married this tempter of time? Yes! Absolutely yes. So I live with it and remind myself how lucky I am the majority of the time.

That reminder works better some days than others. When we are going somewhere I don't want to go, I feel more and more like she is setting me up. You see, I'm not what you'd call a people person. I like people fine. I like doing things with friends, and I can be friendly with cashiers and waiters. But what I am completely uncomfortable with is mingling at a gathering. Even at a gathering of people I know well, like a church Christmas party, I'm uncomfortable until I make my way to a corner where I'll have a fine time talking to another introvert. But waiting to go to a gathering where I won't know most of the people there makes me almost risk a shaved head. What if there isn't a corner to hide in?

"Whatcha thinking?" asked Alice as she climbed into my truck.

"Would you believe me if I told you I was just wondering about the architecture of the O'Briens' home?"

"I wouldn't believe it if anyone else said it," she said. "You aren't going to *inspect* their home are you? This is social, remember."

"You look nice," I told her.

We arrived at the O'Brien home in Johnson City at twelve-forty. I was relieved to see no other cars in the driveway or out front. So was Alice.

"See," she said in her soothing voice, "we're not late."

I didn't say what I was thinking.

The O'Brien home was not the lavish showpiece I had expected from how Lionel and Ingrid had dressed in St. Lucia. From the look outside I'd have guessed it was a four-or five-bedroom house. Inside it was roomy and well lit, which I knew Alice would like. Natural light is her number-one decorating objective. It was also furnished in a rustic farm style that me feel like I could sit anywhere without upsetting something.

Lionel answered the door and took us through the kitchen, where Alice stayed to talk with Ingrid. Lionel fixed us all an orange-and-cranberry-juice concoction and then led me to the dining room.

"Sit anywhere," he told me as he sat his juice at the end of the table nearest the kitchen.

I sat down on the side but at the other end. It didn't dawn on me that he might have expected me to sit next to him or that Alice would have preferred the other side of the table because it faced the window. If given a choice, I would always pick the chair facing the door and where no one could sneak up behind me. I have never had anyone sneak up behind me, but like every guy my age, I did grow up on cowboy movies. Cowboy movies taught me to be kind to women, to be suspicious of anyone in a black hat, and to never sit with your back to the door.

"I hope you like Brunswick stew," said Ingrid as she made her entrance.

"He'll eat anything," said Alice, following close behind.

"It just seems that way because I married such a good cook."

Alice sat next to me and smiled, and then to Ingrid she said, "His definition of a good cook is someone who puts onions in his food."

"There's onions in the Brunswick stew," said Ingrid, "but I can add more if you'd like."

"Quit picking on him, you two," piped in Lionel.

"Yeah," I said. "Give me some slack. I'm wearing socks."

The reference to our first encounter in St. Lucia brought an immediate laugh from everyone in the room, which really helped me relax.

"'Worry not,' Jesus said," quoted Lionel, shifting his body into a more erect frame, "about what you eat or what you wear."

I recognized the quote from the Sermon on the Mount. Patting my stomach I added, "Not worrying about what I eat is why I *have* to worry about what I wear."

I had used the line before. It had gotten a good laugh the first time

I used it, so I was ready. This laughter relaxed me even more, but it didn't last long. The detective arrived.

She's a detective? She looked lost as she followed her brother into the dining room. I'm not sure what I expected—a female version of Sam Spade from *The Maltese Falcon*—but whatever I expected, it wasn't her. She was petite, like her mother, but she didn't carry herself with the same confidence her mother did. She didn't look tough or clever; she didn't even look observant. She was cute. A cute little girl. How is a cute little girl supposed to help me?

I managed to get through all the introductions and handshakes and chitchat, but it felt unreal—like an out-of-body experience. I hated not knowing what I'm supposed to do, and I hated that it unnerved me so. I looked at Alice hoping she'd notice, although there wasn't anything she could do. She hadn't noticed. She was in the full swing of the banter—telling stories, having a good time.

Me, I'm in the beginning of the most embarrassing episode of my life, and I'm trapped in the home of some people I don't know very well but might really need before this is all over. I could have handled all of that and at least relaxed enough to enjoy lunch, but this cutie detective made everything too much for me. *Am I expected to hire her? I can't imagine hiring her. Does she know they've recommended her to me?* I hadn't thought to ask that. I looked back at Alice. It wasn't fair that I resented her for not thinking of it either, but I did. I nervously readjusted the napkin in my lap. When I looked up I was looking straight at the cutie detective sitting directly across from me, watching.

Oh great, she's studying me. I squirmed back in my chair a bit. *What's she doing?* I was confused. I thought she'd be trying to get me to hire her, but she's not looking like she was trying to close the deal. The way she was studying me made me feel the same way I do when a woman treats me like I'm ogling her, even though I'm not.

"So how did you guys meet?" asked the brother.

"We met in high school," Alice told him.

Panic struck me. I knew the story she was about to tell. *Don't tell that story,* I pleaded with her through my eyes, but she didn't look at me at all. *She's gonna tell that story.* I don't mind people knowing that story, I don't mind it at all, but I don't want to be there when they hear it. It makes me sound different from how I feel. It sounds like she's talking about someone else. *Don't tell that story!* I shouted silently, but it was too late.

I felt the breath leave my chest and my shoulders sink as I turned away in defeat. I didn't mean to look at the daughter again, but she was right there across from me. Still watching. Still studying.

The rest of the meal was a blur. I think I had two bowls of the Brunswick stew, but I can't be sure. I just wanted it to be over. I was thankful that the brother took all the attention. Did he really have a moneymaking scheme selling "111 in 01/01/01" T-shirts to people born in 1990?

"They'll all be graduating from college soon, so it would be a perfect gift," he told us as the dishes were being cleared.

I just wanted to go home.

"You said you're from Bristol," began the brother, focusing on me again.

I don't remember telling him that, but I don't remember much about lunch. Maybe Alice told him.

I nodded.

"Well, what do you do?" he asked.

"I work for the city," I told him.

"Bristol?"

"Kingsport," corrected Alice. "He works for the city of Kingsport."

The brother lit up when Alice told him that. "Say, Jack," he said, pointing at me, "do you know a guy named Alexander Sebastian Stout?"

CHAPTER 28

Monday Morning
at Betty's Stockyard Café

"I'M SORRY I'M LATE," SAID NATTIE as she stepped out of the car. After their discovery of each other's identity the day before, she agreed to meet Jack for breakfast in Kingsport. It was a much earlier appointment than she wanted, but she couldn't say no—especially after Kevin had nearly given him a heart attack by asking if he knew Alexander Sebastian Stout.

Jack was sitting on the porch of Betty's Stockyard Café reading a newspaper. She had Google Mapped the café and had mistakenly assumed she'd see it as she drove by. She had seen the stockyard itself, so after driving five minutes past it, she turned around and returned to the stockyard and found Betty's tucked behind some trees, hiding it from the road.

"Thank you for agreeing to meet me here," said Jack as he stood. "You're not late. I'm early."

Jack held the door open for her to enter first, but once inside she hesitated. The layout threw her off. She had expected tables. She had expected a private conversation, which amplified her expectation for tables. Instead of tables there was a counter that paralleled three of the walls; the kitchen was behind the back wall.

Jack led her to the left and took the last two seats near the back corner. A single waitress worked the entire counter. She seemed to know everyone in the room.

"You need a menu, honey?" asked the waitress, whose nametag said "Ava."

"Do we?" Nattie asked Jack.

"Oh, I know what he's havin', but this is your first time with us."

"What's he having?" asked Nattie.

"Scrambled eggs, biscuits and gravy, and tomatoes," smiled Ava. "Here," handing Nattie a menu, "I'll let you look this over while I get your drinks."

"Orange juice," said Jack.

"Me, too," said Nattie, "and I'll have two eggs over medium and toast—wheat if you have it."

Ava nodded as she wrote down their orders. As she passed the paper through to the kitchen, an older gentleman entered and circled to the other side of the café.

"Eustace," Ava called out. The old man waved with the back of his hand.

Nattie looked down the row. As near as she could tell, she was the only one who didn't order the biscuits and gravy or the tomatoes.

"I, umm—" Jack frowned. "I, umm—" he repeated. Shaking his head, he finally said, "I hope I didn't offend you yesterday when your brother said I was a suspect in your investigation." He looked, for the first time, directly into Nattie's eyes.

Nattie met his gaze but said nothing.

"I know you don't know if I'm innocent or not, but it was still a shock to hear that you are already working against me." He huffed a laugh. "My wife wanted me to hire you to find out who really stole that stuff."

"Are you innocent?" she asked.

He recoiled from her. "That was blunt," he said, righting himself on his stool.

"I've been called that before," smiled Nattie. "Are you?"

"Am I blunt?"

"Are you innocent?"

Ava returned with their orange juices.

"Thanks," Jack said to Ava. "Yes," he added as soon as Ava moved on. He turned to look at her, "Do you believe me?"

"You're a suspect, but there are others, so the truth is I can't completely believe you until I find out who's guilty. I'm sorry if that bothers you."

"It's the truth," replied Jack. "I appreciate you telling *me* the truth. It might have made me feel better for the moment if you had said you believed me, but soon enough I'd have realized you had no reason to believe me."

"Look, Mr. Stout," Nattie said gently, "you can count on me to search for the truth. That's what I do. So if you know you are innocent, then you know you have nothing to fear from my investigation. If you know you're innocent, then I promise you there will come a time when I will know it, too."

He was still studying her face when Ava came with their breakfasts.

"Look okay?" asked Ava.

Jack nodded yes. Nattie looked down and noticed two large slices of beautiful red tomato on the side of her plate. When she looked up Ava said, "I added those," she waved her hand as she left. "You're new."

"I love places like this," Nattie announced.

"Mmmm," agreed Jack. His mouth was already too full to speak.

They ate in silence. Jack finished first, although his was the larger meal.

"Why don't you tell me anything you think would help me figure out who broke into the Holmes home?" suggested Nattie as she spread a thin layer of apple butter on her toast.

"I'll be honest with you," began Jack. "This has really thrown me for a loop. They questioned me four years ago. I don't even think I was a suspect then. But now, out of the blue, I'm a suspect."

"Why do you think you're a suspect?"

"I suppose it could be argued that I knew Heart Construction was going to do a shoddy job, and if I had been the inspector for more than just the structure, then I'd have known exactly how that safe room was vulnerable." He took a deep breath. "Whoever broke into that house knew exactly where it was vulnerable."

"And you would have been someone who would have known that," clarified Nattie.

"If I had inspected that room at each step of construction, it would not have been built that way."

"But you weren't."

"Nope," he said with a shake of his head for punctuation.

"Who was?"

"No one."

Nattie's eyebrows clamped together, and she tipped her head to the left.

"I was there for the foundation and the structure, and then the city manager pulled me off the job."

"Why would he do that?"

"I advised him to. That's why. We'd had trouble with that hack of a contractor many, many times. I knew that unless I could camp out there twenty-four hours a day, he'd pull something."

"You're on record telling the city manager that?"

"Yeah."

"I'd like a copy of that, if you don't mind."

"It's an email," he said. "I'm sure I can find it."

"And his response, too," she added.

"That was a memo, but I know right where it is. I had to testify at the original investigation. I still have everything I put together for that."

"Great."

"Does that make you believe me a little more?" he asked.

Nattie smiled. "Who else would have known how vulnerable that room was?"

Jack snorted. "Everyone who had ever had any dealings with Heart Construction."

Nattie looked at him. "Do you want to help me find out who did this?"

"Of course."

"Then I need you to be more specific than that. Maybe everyone knew the contractor was a hack, but who would have known specifically how those walls were vulnerable?"

Jack thought a moment. "I heard that the way they broke in was by cutting a section of the wall out with a chain saw. Is that accurate?"

"That's what the report I read said."

"Then whoever did it was either lucky or they knew the material was cuttable and that there was no electrical in that wall."

"Okay," said Nattie, "that's better. That's going to be a smaller list. Any ideas?"

"That's interesting," Jack said, looking off into space. "I watched that construction go together for the framing of the walls and the cutting in of the electrical. If he had used the material he was supposed to for those exterior walls, then no one could have chainsawed their way in. I wasn't there to see that, but like I said, I did see the wiring go in. Whoever cut that wall open had to know where the wiring was."

"At my house, all the outlets are about the same distance from the floor. Is that standard? I mean, wouldn't most construction people know where the wiring was?"

"The horizontal wiring is generally going to be a foot off the floor, but you wouldn't be able to tell exactly where the floor was from the outside. Besides, the vertical wiring could be anywhere."

It was Nattie's turn to look into outer space.

"Is that helpful?" asked Jack.

"It's a puzzle piece," answered Nattie. "It's too early to tell where it fits, but it's an interesting piece."

Jack nodded. He closed his eyes and took a slow breath, "I'm not sure how this works, but. . . ."

"Mr. Stout," interrupted Nattie.

"Call me 'Jack,' please."

"Jack, my mother told me you were thinking of hiring me. You don't need to do that. I'm already going to do whatever it is that I would do if you hired me."

He studied her again.

"I'm already working on finding out who took that artwork."

"Does that mean you'll tell me what's going on?"

"I'll tell you what, Jack. I will keep you informed about what I can, okay? But even if I was working for you, I wouldn't just tell you everything that was going on. If I'm following a lead that involves someone else, it wouldn't be right to tell you anything about that person until I know something is for sure."

He nodded.

"But I have to tell you something else. I'm not the only one investigating this."

"I know," Jack said. "I've got a meeting in a few days with someone named Nate or Nathaniel or something."

"Nathan Moreland," said Nattie.

"Yeah, that sounds right. Do you know him?"

"I do," she said. "He's my ex-husband."

CHAPTER 29

Monday Morning at Manna

KEVIN AND KNOX WERE SITTING IN THE WINDOW SEAT when Nattie walked into Manna Bagel.

Kevin made sure Nattie could see him look at his watch. "Ten-thirty is kinda late for you, isn't it?"

"We," she said with a roll of her eyes, "had a doctor's appointment this morning."

"'We,'" repeated Knox, her pitch climbing higher as she drew the word out the way only a southerner could.

"Nathan and I."

"Did it go okay?" asked Knox.

"The doctor's appointment went great," said Nattie.

"I can tell," said Kevin as he rolled his eyes toward Knox.

"The appointment went well, really. I'm just still steaming over what he told me in the parking lot afterward."

"Well, Sis, have a sit down and tell us all about it."

Nattie glanced down at the chair as Kevin slid it away from the table with his foot. "Let me go get a coffee first."

"I got ya." It was Nathan's voice, but it still made her jump. He had come in through the back door and snuck up behind her.

Nattie snapped, "What are you doing here?"

He spread his hands and then looked at Kevin and then Knox and then Nattie. "It's Monday morning. We always meet at Manna on Monday morning."

"*We* do," snarled Nattie, "but you don't want to be part of the team anymore. Right?"

"Wrong," he answered back, his voice wobbling unconvincingly.

"'Wrong,'" she repeated in a snooty teacher voice.

"What I said was that I had new information about the building inspector and I didn't want *you* pulling me off *my* investigation."

"Your investigation," repeated Nattie. "Did you get a license and start your own agency since Friday?"

"You know, Natalie, this isn't the most attractive side of you."

Natalie scowled. "Did you, in your wildest dreams, think I was trying to be *attractive?*"

Nathan pulled back. "Look, Nattie, I know you have every right to be pissed at me, but you're way out of line now. I don't have a license or an agency, but I did bring this case to you. We all stand to make a lot of money with this case, no matter who solves it, but I don't see what's wrong with me wanting to follow my own leads."

Nattie glared at him.

Kevin and Knox busied themselves looking at something on a menu that they had seen hundreds of times.

"What?" asked Nathan.

"I said I didn't think the building inspector was a good lead, and you said—" she paused, put her finger to her lips, and looked up as if looking for an answer. "Let me see, what was it you said to that?"

Nathan stared at her.

"You told me to take my advice and shove it."

Frowning, Nathan stated, "I never said that."

"Just . . . go," said Nattie slowly, emphasizing each word. She didn't wait for an answer but brushed past him on the way to get her own coffee.

"As you wish," he said through clenched teeth, making sure she could not hear.

Kevin and Knox watched Nathan retreat through the back door.

"What was that about?" asked Kevin as Nathan reached the exit.

"His ego took a beating in the counseling session this morning, but that's not what's bugging him. I told him he'd be better off focusing on the contractor instead of the building inspector."

"I guess he didn't like that," stated Knox.

"I guess not," agreed Nattie.

"Does Nathan know you already met with Jack?" asked Kevin.

Nattie held up two fingers.

"That's right," Kevin said, pointing at her. "You met him this morning, too, didn't you? How'd that go?"

Nodding her head slowly, Nattie considered her answer before saying, "It went well. I'm pretty sure he's not our guy."

"So, if Nathan keeps going after him," observed Knox, "he'll be wasting his time."

"True," agreed Nattie, "but sometimes I consider it a victory if I don't let him waste *my* time."

"So, are you going after the contractor then?" asked Kevin.

"I guess I'll have to, but he's not my primary," said Nattie.

"It's the lawyer guy, isn't it?" asked Knox.

Nodding her head, Nattie said, "For now."

"I think you might want to reevaluate that," suggested Kevin.

"You got some info?"

"I know how Avery Heart's ex-wife paid for that expensive house in Alexandria." Kevin smiled sardonically.

"Is it a secret?" asked Nattie sarcastically, annoyed to have had to ask.

"Shannon Heart's sister, Shelia Evans, sold three hundred thousand dollars' worth of art prints at an auction in Philadelphia." The smile stayed on his face while his eyebrows lifted and he leaned across the table. "Five weeks later, Shannon Heart put a quarter of a mil down on her house."

Nattie leaned back in her chair and stared out the window toward State Street.

"I guess that puts them on the list," spouted Kevin.

"Yeah, it will," agreed Nattie. "How hard would it be to get a list of the prints they sold in Philadelphia?"

"Shouldn't be hard at all."

"Good. Let's get that list and check it against the list we got from Federation Fidelity. We do have that list, don't we?"

Kevin frowned.

"Nathan has that list, doesn't he?"

"We shoulda made copies of all that stuff," observed Kevin.

"I'm sure Nathan will let you copy that list," said Knox softly.

"I'm sure he would, but I'm sure we can get one from Presly Holmes, too. That will give me a conversation starter when I call on him tomorrow." Nattie turned to Knox. "You can go with me if you want."

CHAPTER 30

Meeting Nathan [Jack]

IT WAS MY CHOICE, SO I CHOSE TO MEET HIM at the Hibbert-Davis Coffee Shop. I for sure didn't want to meet him at the office or on a job site, so a coffee shop it had to be. Kingsport has a bunch of coffee shops, but this is my favorite because of the building. It used to be the city garage, so it's huge. It has a huge ceiling and a huge wall at one end of glass-paned garage doors large enough to drive in buses and trucks for servicing.

The giant fireplace in the middle of the room was nice to stare at when you just wanted to get outside of your own head. Outside my own head is where I went. I had come an hour early and brought some paperwork to set in front of me while I waited. I really did intend on getting that done as I waited, but the fire took me away. I don't really know where I went. I just know I wasn't there.

I came back when the phone rang. It was Alice.

"Hey," I said.

"You okay?"

"Yeah, why?"

"You let your phone ring a long time before you answered it."

"I was thinking."

"You were gone, weren't you?"

Sometimes it's annoying how well she can read me, but right then it felt reassuring.

"I was," I admitted.

"Doug called looking for you."

Last week I didn't want to think about being blamed for that robbery, but now I didn't want to think about being unemployed.

"What did he say?" I asked her.

"He said he's coming into town and wants to do breakfast later this week. I said you'd love that."

I smiled. When I worked for him, we'd meet for breakfast every Friday morning. He introduced me to Betty's Stockyard Café.

"Did you give him my phone number?"

"I did, but I told him to call you this afternoon. I didn't tell him you were in a meeting this morning with a PI."

"Thanks."

"He was calling from the airport, so he won't be calling back today. He said he'd meet you on Thursday morning unless he heard from you. I have his number."

"Did he say where or when?"

"When I asked him that, he just laughed and said you'd know."

And I did. It was the first really relaxing moment I'd had so far that day. Then it was over as I noticed the guy in the doorway. He was scouting out the room like he was looking for someone. I knew right away it was probably me.

He looked right at me and smiled. I guess my disguise as a CPA didn't fool him.

"I gotta go," I told Alice.

"Relax," she said softly. "You'll be fine."

I knew she was right, but my stomach was still a knot. I managed to say "thanks" just as the PI reached my table.

"Hey," he said, "are you Alexander Stout?"

147

"Jack," I said.

He sat down across from me. He was what I'd call an average guy: six foot, medium build, dark hair, and brown eyes. But he was slicked up—expensive clothes, expensive haircut, gaudy watch.

"I'm Nathan Moreland," he told me. "We talked on the phone the other day. Like I said, I'm reinvestigating the Holmes art robbery."

"And I'm a suspect."

He grinned. "Everyone is a suspect at this point."

I faked a smile.

"Let's talk about that robbery."

"Okay," I told him. "What do you what to know?"

"I want to know if you robbed that house."

I laughed. I couldn't help it. The question was so amateurish that the knot in my stomach disappeared.

"Nope," I proclaimed. "Anything else?"

He grinned again.

"If I were guilty, do you think I would have told you?"

He shrugged and kept grinning.

The guy is a dude. I felt guilty—no, make that silly—for being nervous to meet with him.

"If you got no more questions for me, then I have one for you."

"I may have a few more questions, but go ahead. What do you want to ask me?"

"Why me?" I asked.

"You were the building inspector. . . ."

"I *am* the building inspector," I corrected him. I wasn't going to let that pass.

He rolled his eyes. What a snot. Every time he opened his mouth I got less and less nervous and more and more pissed off. Maybe it was his haircut.

"Yes, you are the building inspector, but you *were* the building inspector when that robbery took place."

"And that's why I was suspect then. Why am I a suspect now?"

"Everyone who was a suspect then is a suspect now." He leaned back and smugly added, "Why are you so concerned? Do you have something to hide?"

Right now I'm hiding my curiosity about how many times I could hit you before you cried. I thought to myself before saying, "What I am asking you, sir, is this: Is there some new reason the spotlight has turned in my direction?"

"You mean the coins?" he asked.

"Coins? What about the coins?"

"You tell me about the coins," he said, leaning forward again.

"I don't know anything about any coins."

"Nobody's told you that some of the coins from the robbery were discovered?"

"Yeah, I know that much. Up on Bays Mountain, right?"

"What else do you not know?"

I did know I wanted to make him cry. "I know—make that, I think—they were found this spring. That's when I got a letter from the city attorney."

"That's right. It was at the end of April."

"Okay."

"Now I have a question for you, Mr. Stout. When exactly was it that you took a luxury vacation?"

My stomach knotted again. He thinks I financed our St. Lucia trip with stolen coins. "I think you already know the answer to that." I spoke slowly so that my voice wouldn't crack.

"Beginning of May," he said immediately.

"We saved for years for that trip. My financial records are spotless." This was bravado, of course, because I had paid for that trip with gold coins I had been buying from the mint ever since we paid off our daughter Sally's wedding.

"I'll be asking for those records if you don't mind."

I minded. But I'd cooperate when it came down to it.

"But," he said, leaning back again, "financial records can be doctored."

"So, I go on a once-in-a-lifetime trip with my wife, and that makes me a suspect for a robbery four years ago. I'll bet there are a thousand people in the Tri-Cities who have gone on luxury vacations between the time of that robbery and my trip."

"Maybe. But how many took luxury vacations between the time of yours and the reappearance of those coins?"

"That's a coincidence."

"Do you know anything about that new aviary shelter on Bays Mountain?"

"I was the inspector," I admitted. "That was in 2010."

"Yes," he said. "Just after the Holmes break-in."

"Is that where the coins were found?"

"The coins were found just off a path about fifty yards from the aviary." His eyes narrowed. "But there was a hole found right behind it."

"So, you think I robbed that house and buried the coins behind the aviary, then four years later I went back and dug them up so I could go on a vacation."

"You said it," he said. "I didn't."

"What am I supposed to have done with all the other loot?"

"I was hoping you'd tell me, but I didn't expect you to."

"You got nothing," I boasted. "Those are all coincidences."

"Maybe so," he preened, "but that's not all I have."

I assumed he was bluffing.

"I have a witness," he said.

CHAPTER 31

Tuesday: Presly Holmes

KAYLEIGH BUCKNER WASN'T IN PRESLY HOLMES'S waiting room when they arrived, so Nattie and Knox walked directly into his office. The door was open, which Nattie took to be an invitation; they were expected, after all. So she led the way, and Knox followed close behind. She immediately began to rethink that decision once inside.

"Git away from that car," screamed a very tall man. He was leaning forward against the window overlooking Broad Street with his hands spread out on the wall above the window. With each word he yelled, he propelled himself forward up off his heels and against the glass. *"You better run, you little pukes,"* he continued, pounding his palms against the wall above his head.

Nattie stood frozen, not so much in fear, but as if she was an inadvertent and completely unwilling witness. She was embarrassed for the big man, and although his performance was not intended for an audience, he had done nothing to hide it either. If she could have done so quietly enough, she would have backed out of the room and pretended not to have heard or seen anything.

"What's the matter?" asked Knox from behind as she noticed Nattie hesitating.

The huge man spun around with more quickness than a man of his size could typically muster. Once facing them he crouched and spread his arms apart the way a linebacker would. His body said he was ready for action. The bulge in his eyes and the unnatural exposure of only his lower teeth said he'd enjoy the action as well.

Nattie held her palms out. "We're your ten o'clock."

It only took a second, but when he flipped into his charming-lawyer mode, the metamorphosis was astonishing.

"I'm Presly Holmes," he announced, still speaking loudly. He crossed the room in a couple of strides, his open hand outstretched. Gone was the crazed look, replaced by a chubby-cheeked baby face and a smile that would make a furniture salesman jealous. "My mother was a huge Elvis Presley fan," he explained, winking, "but she couldn't spell to save her life."

His handshake was surprisingly gentle, and he held on while looking Nattie up and down. He was not too concerned with how obvious he was being.

Nattie, ever uncomfortable with any scrutiny, was especially uncomfortable with this kind, to which her choice of modest attire attested. She was wearing loose-fitting, androgynous pants and a polo shirt. She admired the freedom Knox had in wearing what she wore, but Nattie could never have done so herself. Knox dressed as a twenty-something who was completely comfortable with her body.

"I'm sorry about that," he said, pointing his thumb over his shoulder toward the window. "That canary-yellow Jaguar out there is mine. Every high school kid in town wants a picture of his girlfriend sitting on the hood."

"I'm Nattie Moreland from Bristol. This is Knox DeVilla. We're here about the 2009 burglary of your home."

He took Knox's hand next. "I think I've heard you sing," he said. He didn't let her hand go, either. As his eyes made their way up and down her body, he smiled a spideresque smile. "Were you at

O'Mannon's on the last night of Rhythm & Roots a couple of years ago?"

"I was," said Knox, turning slightly to her left. "But it was last year, not two years ago. Were you there, too?"

Are you flirting? Seriously? Nattie, for the first time, noticed the similarity between her mother, Ingrid, and Knox. The realization moved her to another thought: *Are all of us doomed to marry our parents?* Nattie had not only married an alcoholic, like her father, but one with the same name: Nathan. If Kevin married Knox, he'd be marrying someone very much like his mother.

"No," he answered, laughing. "It was a wild guess." Then he winked at Nattie. "I'm just kidding. I was there. You were great."

"Thank you," said Knox, tugging her hand away.

"We're here about the 2009 burglary of your home," Nattie repeated, feeling a bit like an intruder.

Turning an eye toward Nattie he said, "You're that female detective from Bristol, right? Nikita MacMartinez."

She handed him a card. "That's Natasha McMorales," she corrected. "And that isn't really my name. It's the agency name. I'm Nattie Moreland."

"Welcome. Come on in and sit down," he said, stepping to the side and gesturing them forward with a sweep of his hand. As Knox followed Nattie farther into the room, he placed his hand on her back and caressed her as he directed her to the empty chair facing his desk. Nattie was standing next to the other chair but didn't sit until Presly began circling his desk.

"What can I do for you?" he asked as he sat.

"We represent Federation Fidelity," began Nattie. "We're trying to recover some of the art stolen from your home four years ago."

He nodded.

"Is there anything you could tell us that might help us?"

He shrugged. "Do you already have the police reports?"

153

Nattie nodded.

"How about the insurance reports?"

"We have the report from their investigation, but we don't have copies of the original policy—"

"The original policy," he interrupted Nattie. "What do you need that for?"

That hit a nerve, observed Nattie. "I don't know what I need. I just know I don't have that. And I don't have a detailed list of the missing items."

"Really," he said in a raised voice.

"The list I received from Federation Fidelity does not have the kind of detail that I was hoping the original policy would have had. Surely there was an appraisal."

"Surely there was," he said, smiling.

Go ahead and mock me now, thought Nattie as she smiled innocently at him.

Knox, who had been sitting stoically as was her custom, suddenly lurched forward, leaning her right elbow on the edge of the desk: "Why don't you stop being such a jerk-wad and just answer the question?"

It took a moment for the shock to wear off enough for Nattie to redirect her attention back to Presly Holmes. His attention was still entirely focused on Knox. He had a blank, hypnotized expression.

"Well?" demanded Knox, still leaning on the desk.

The shock wore off his face, and the baby-faced grin reappeared. "Feisty. I like that."

"Save it," returned Knox without flinching.

He met her stare while he picked up a manila envelope from the left corner of his desk. He handed the envelope to Nattie. "Everything you asked for is in there—everything, that is, but the original contract."

"When can we expect that?" asked Nattie.

He turned his full attention to Nattie. "I'll have to find it first. And now, if you don't mind, I have other matters to tend to."

"I don't mind," said Knox sharply.

Nattie stood up and tucked the envelope under her left arm. "Thank you for your time. I'll let you know if we need anything else."

"Yeah," he said with a snort. "You do that."

Huffing, Knox stood and walked to the door where she waited for Nattie.

"What's with her?" he laughed. "She one of those hippie *feminazis?*"

"If what that means is seeing through your BS, then we all are."

As Nattie walked toward the door Knox said, "Don't sweat him, Nattie. He belongs in the pen with the other pigs."

CHAPTER 32

Wednesday Afternoon: Nathan and Nattie

"HEY, NATTIE," YELLED KEVIN FROM HIS DESK.

Nattie clenched her teeth. Being yelled at—summoned—set her on edge. The assumption when someone yelled at you like that was that whatever they had in mind for you was more important than whatever you were doing at that moment.

"*What?*" she screamed back at him, but only in her imagination.

"You're gonna wanna come out here," he announced, this time with his head peeking around the door frame.

Nattie put her pencil in her mouth and tucked the pad of paper she was working on in her desk. She didn't want anyone to see her doodling. On the page she had written Avery Heart's name in one top corner and Presly Holmes's name in the other. Jack's name went on one side of the bottom and a question mark on the other. *Too many suspects,* she said to herself as she shut the drawer.

As Nattie cleared her office she stopped suddenly. In the waiting room stood Janice Chafin from the Enchanted Florist. Janice's arms held the largest collection of daisies Nattie had ever seen outside of a field. They were in some sort of cardboard tray.

"Do you have a place for these?" asked Janice.

"Here you go," said Nattie, taking some magazines off the end table.

"They'll need some water," Janice said as she put down the flowers.

"I got it," said Kevin, dashing around Janice toward the utility closet at the back of the waiting room.

As Kevin rumbled around in the other room, Nattie stepped closer to the flowers. They were in a large cardboard box about five inches high. Nattie moved some flowers around to see what they were held in. "Is that—"

"Mason jars," said Janice. "This guy came in with a brand-new case of Mason jars. He had cut the top off the box and he said he wanted me to fill all of the jars with fresh flowers."

"What guy?" asked Nattie, although she was pretty sure she knew the answer.

"I have a card," said Janice, "somewhere here in my pocket."

They both jumped as something crashed in the utility closet. The crash was followed by Kevin returning with a watering can.

"Found it," he boasted, holding the can up such that a short stream of water hit him in the chest.

Janice handed Nattie the card. "Enjoy," she said, excusing herself.

Nattie opened the note. It read, "I was wrong." It wasn't signed. It didn't need to be.

The door hadn't closed all the way after Janice left when Nathan came in. He stood in the doorway waiting to be noticed, which took a while as Kevin was cleaning up the utility room and Nattie was standing over the box of daisy jars with the watering can. Her back was to the door.

"Did you read the note?" Nathan finally asked.

Nattie eyed him.

"I was wrong," he said sheepishly.

"Are you apologizing, Nathan?"

"I am. I never should have gone off on my own like that, and I never should have talked to you that way."

"No, you shouldn't have."

"Can we talk?"

Nattie didn't answer right away, so he continued. "It's about the case. I think I just messed up."

"Come on back," she said, leading the way to her office.

Once they were settled, Nathan seated on one side of the desk and Nattie behind it, she asked, "What's up?"

"I met with the building inspector," he began. "He's our guy, I know it. But I think I played it wrong."

"First things first, Nathan. What makes you think he's our guy?"

He stood back up. Pacing he said, "First of all, he was one of the original suspects because he knew what the vulnerabilities were in that home." He stopped in front of her desk and placed both hands flat on top. Leaning forward he added, "Now, I know he wasn't charged last time, but neither was anyone else." He tapped his finger. "One of those original guys got away with it back then by putting all that art away for later." Then he stood, saying, "And now some of those coins have shown up." He paused, staring at her while drumming the fingers of his right arm against his left bicep.

"Which one of your suspects do you suppose is most connected to where those coins turned up?"

"It's just a wild guess, mind you, but it's not the building inspector, is it?"

"You know damn well it is," he bluffed.

"I'll bite. What are the connections?"

"One," he began, holding up his index finger, "the coins were buried near an aviary he inspected. It was built around the same time as the robbery."

"Okay."

"Two, the coins were dug up just before he went on a luxury vacation."

She nodded.

"And finally, we have a witness who saw him on Bays Mountain the day before the coins were discovered."

Wow, thought Nattie, *I didn't see that coming.* After having met with Jack she was sure he wasn't guilty. Her gut instincts were usually more reliable than this. "You make a good case," she conceded.

"But I think I spooked him."

"Why?"

"Well," he huffed, "I didn't do it on purpose."

"Not why did you do it?" she corrected. "Why do you think you did it?"

He frowned. "He asked me why I was talking to him, so I told him everything I just told you."

"He already knew all that, didn't he?"

"I don't think so. He seemed pretty shocked when I told him there was a witness."

"Don't worry about it," she reassured him. "Hiram used to say that sometimes you have to rattle the cage and see who barks. That's all you did, really."

He smiled. "Just rattling his cage."

"FYI, we've got some new evidence implicating Avery Heart, too. His ex-wife used some art prints to pay cash for a home in Alexandria."

"Are you going to go rattle her cage?"

"Probably," she said as she stood. She stared at him until she had his full attention. "Speaking of cage rattling, if you ever talk to me that way again, we are done."

"I was just—" he began.

"Excuse me," she interrupted sternly. "I'm not interested in hearing an excuse."

"How about an explanation?"

"Not interested. I just want to know that you heard me."

He nodded. He wasn't pacing anymore.

"Thank you for the flowers, but in the future, if you need to apologize for something, then I'd prefer it if you'd just walk in here and say what you have to say."

"Apologize like a man," he emphasized.

"I didn't say that," she said, thinking, *but that's what I meant.*

CHAPTER 33

Doug Hout's Return [Jack]

I GOT TO BETTY'S BEFORE DOUG DID. I was hoping seven-fifteen would do it, but I wasn't sure. He was always a very early riser. I waited for him on the porch. I wanted a private conversation with him, at least to start, before we sat at the bar inside. I didn't want an audience when we talked about my situation, and I'm pretty sure he wasn't going to want one when we talked about his, either.

Doug had retired and left Kingsport ten years ago. He was only sixty-three at the time, but his wife, Franny, was on disability with lung cancer, so early retirement was arranged and they headed off to Arizona. Franny had been in remission, but it came back a year ago and took her six months later. I had talked to him on the phone once since then, but this would be the first time I'd seen him in a decade.

I had my head down, reading Joe Tennis's new book, *Haunts of Virginia's Blue Ridge Highlands,* when Doug drove up in what looked like the same old brown Datsun pickup truck he had driven when he left town.

"Hey, Jocko, whatcha know?" he greeted me as he got out of his truck.

Same ol' Doug. He was the only one who ever called me "Jocko," and only when he was in a good mood, which was almost never. His hair was a little more silver and his face quite a bit more weathered, but other than that he was the same.

"I'll tell you something I didn't know," I said, standing up. "I didn't know you could find another truck the color of dog crap."

"Hell," he sneered, "that's not another truck. That's the same truck I've had for twenty years." He pounded on the roof. "Two hundred thousand miles," he bragged.

"Did you just drive that antique from Arizona?"

"'Course I did," he strained to say as he ambled up the couple of steps.

By the time he got to me he was breathing hard.

"I thought you'd be in one of those new hybrids," I said as he gripped my hand. His hand felt bonier than I remember.

"I just might," he said after a deep breath. "But there's still a lot of life in that thing."

"You just gonna drive it until it falls apart?"

"Yep."

I clapped him gently on the shoulder. He didn't look like he could take much of a punch anymore. There was a time when he'd taken a punch from half the contractors in Kingsport. The word was that he was too slow to get out of the way but too ornery to fall down. "Are you real hungry, or can we jaw a little out here first?"

"What's on your mind?" he asked, sitting down.

Now that I'd seen him move around and stood next to him, I knew he wasn't the same old Doug. When he left he was just a bit shorter than me. I'm six-foot-two, so I'd have put him at six feet. But I'd be surprised if he was five-foot-eight now, and he moved like it hurt to walk.

"I just wanted to say how sorry I was to hear about Franny passing."

He nodded and looked down.

"She was a real nice lady," I added.

"Better than I deserved, that's for sure."

"Probably," I agreed, "but I know you were good to her."

He looked up. His eyes were a little glossy and a little pink. "Thanks."

"Where ya' staying?" I asked.

"I got a niece who lives here. She's the only family I got now."

"What about your daughter?" I asked. I thought his daughter, Kayleigh, lived in Kingsport. As soon as I asked the question I regretted it. The last thing I wanted to do was remind him of another loss.

"Kayleigh," he said, "is actually our niece. Franny and I raised her after my sister died. She is more like a daughter to me."

"I didn't know that."

"Yeah, and ever since Franny died, she's been trying to get me to move back to Kingsport. She told me she'd do anything to git me back here so's she could take care of me." He shook his head slowly. "It is nice. And I'd do anything for her, but I resisted. I can't really abide the thought of being took care of."

"So, why now?" I asked, but I was pretty sure I knew why now. He's here to cover my ass, or worse.

Without making eye contact he said, "I'm not here to replace you, Jack. The new city manager called me last week. He said you were having some PR trouble, and could I come back until this robbery thing is cleaned up?" Then he looked me right in the face. "They picked up Franny's hospital tab, Jack. I had to say yes. But I told him this is a short-term deal. Hell, I'm seventy-three. I don't want your job."

"I know," I told him, but it wasn't like that made me feel better. His presence here made me wonder if my job was up for grabs.

"This is just a bunch of PR BS, isn't it, Jack? I mean, you're innocent."

That last statement sounded like a question to me, especially when he gave me the stink eye after he said it.

163

"Being innocent doesn't keep 'em from screwing with my life."

"Nope. It don't. But being innocent goes a long way to deciding how all this turns out in the end." He patted me on the arm. "Just don't let it get to you."

I smiled at him like I appreciated the advice. *Gee,* I thought, *don't let it get to me. I wish I could.*

"Say, Jack, do you know anything about this Merry-Go-Round project they got going?"

"The carousel?"

"Yeah, that's it. Kayleigh says they're looking for whittlers to work on the animals. I was actually thinking about coming back and apprenticing to one of the whittlers when the city manager called."

It was hard for me to picture Doug Hout being an apprentice to anyone, especially an artist. I'm guessing he'd last about a day and a half before he was telling the artist there were more efficient ways to work. The thought of him getting bossy with a guy holding a knife brought a smile to my face.

"That's a great project," I told him. "The whole city is rallying behind it. They'll be glad to have you."

CHAPTER 34

Nattie Meets Doug at Betty's

SINCE EVEN NATHAN CONCEDED THAT HE WAS NO LONGER going to be effective in dealing with Jack Stout, they agreed to exchange the leads each would follow. Nathan would pursue Shannon Heart and the art prints her sister had sold in Philadelphia. Nattie would follow up with Jack and the coins found on Bays Mountain.

Jack wasn't home the night before when Nattie called. Alice said he'd be at Betty's first thing in the morning, so she was there, too. To Nattie, first thing in the morning meant eight o'clock, so she got there at eight. Jack, however, was nowhere in sight when she stepped inside.

"Sit anywhere, honey," Ava told her. Then she added with an expression of recognition, "Welcome back."

"Do you remember the man I was here with last week?" asked Nattie.

"Jack?"

"Yes. Has he been here yet?"

"Hadn't seen him, but he'll be here. He wouldn't stand you up."

Nattie's shoulders slumped. "He doesn't know I'm looking for him. His wife just told me he'd be here."

"You want some breakfast while you wait?"

Nattie shook her head no.

"Coffee?"

"Please."

As Nattie started scanning the counter for a place to sit, she couldn't help but notice a silver-haired old-timer pointing at the empty chair just to his left.

This is not what I need, she thought.

"You lookin' for Jack Stout?"

"Yes."

"He was here a half hour ago. We had a little get-together on the porch, and then he had to go. He never came inside though."

Nattie settled in next to him. "Is he coming back?"

"Doubt it. But if this is about a building, maybe I could help."

"No. It's more of a personal nature."

The old man eyed her more closely. "Is this about that robbery?"

The question surprised Nattie. "What makes you ask that?"

He grinned. "I figured it was either that or you two were having an affair, and forgive me my manners, but Jocko ain't in your league."

Am I supposed to say "Thank you" to something like that?

"I don't know why y'all are still bothering with him about that. There's no way Jack could have pulled something like that. He's a Boy Scout. I remember once we ate at that German restaurant over in Johnson City and we each thought the other paid. We didn't figure it out until we got back to Kingsport, but I thought Jack was gonna git sick. I was driving and I told him we'd call and tell 'em we'd take care of it next time we were there, but he got in his truck and went right back."

"Who are you?" Nattie asked.

"I'm Douglas Lightfeather Hout," he tipped his head. "Most people call me Doug, but pretty girls like you—"

"Don't call at all," said Ava, who had suddenly appeared with Nattie's coffee.

Doug grinned. "Just 'cause you don't call me, Ava, don't mean other pretty girls don't call."

She looked at Nattie. "Don't take anything he says seriously."

"I'll have you know, I got real serious while I was in Arizona. It's a known fact that arid climates make you serious. Look at how serious all those old photographs of the Navajos are. You never seen one with a big smile, did you?"

"That's what I mean," said Ava. "He'll make stuff up just to see who'll bite on it. If you want anything else, just holler." With that she left.

Doug leaned over to her. "I do like to make stuff up, but I was being serious about Jack. He's as straight an arrow as there is."

Nattie nodded.

"You know, you never told me your name," he said, cutting another piece of meat.

"Nattie Moreland. I'm a PI from Bristol."

"Really?" he asked, sounding shocked.

"Really," she answered.

He grinned a big, toothy grin.

"Do you think it's funny that I'm a PI?"

"Nope, I got no problem with a girl PI," he explained. "I was just remembering all I said about how Jack couldn't have done it. I could've gone a different direction just to git a rise out a ya." He looked square at her. "It's a good thing I didn't do that, huh?"

"As long as you're talking about him, is there anything else you can tell me?"

"I kin tell you this," he said. "I knew hiring Avery Heart was a problem even before they hired him. Hell, I predicted it, but nobody listens to me."

Nattie had to digest that a moment. "I'm sorry. What do you mean you predicted it and nobody listened?"

He shifted back and more toward her in his seat. He was settling in to tell a story he wanted to tell. More than tell it, he wanted to watch his audience listen to it—the way a fisherman savored the telling of the one that got away.

"I was the building inspector here in Kingsport before Jack came. I hired him. So I still know most of the contractors working here. And I still get calls every now and then asking my advice about who to hire for this or that. Anyway, my niece works for that idiot lawyer whose house got robbed."

"Your niece is Kayleigh Buckner."

"Yeah. So she was telling me about that project and I said, 'Whatever y'all do, don't hire Heart. He'll botch it, for sure."

"You told Presly Holmes's receptionist that," clarified Nattie.

"I did. I'm guessing he wishes he had listened to me now."

I'm wondering if he did listen to you, thought Nattie.

CHAPTER 35

Shannon Heart

NATTIE HAD BEEN AT HER DESK DOODLING on a pad of paper. She had abandoned the sheet of paper with her three prime suspects at opposing corners because it had become unreadable. Now she had separate pads for each of the suspects. Every time she thought one suspect had merged ahead of the others, some new piece of information would come along and shift the light somewhere else.

"What I need now is a little luck to come my way," she said out loud, although not loud enough for Kevin to hear from the other room.

"You busy?" Kevin asked from the doorway.

"Nope. Why?"

"'Cause Shannon Heart is here to see you."

Nattie looked down at the Avery Heart pad of paper. Shannon Heart's name was written several times. *If this was a novel,* thought Nattie, *it wouldn't be believable.*

As Nattie put the pads of paper in her drawer, Shannon Heart strode into Nattie's office. She was dressed in black slacks and a sleeveless teal blouse. Her brown hair was cut in a flip that Nattie had only seen on reruns of the *Mary Tyler Moore Show,* and her makeup was conspicuously thick. Other than being out of date, she carried herself with confidence.

"Is this you?" she asked, setting one of Nattie's business cards on the desk.

"It is."

She sat down as Nattie stood, reaching out her hand. The handshake and pleasant introductions were skipped.

"You already know who I am, so let me get right to why I am here."

"Great," said Nattie, retrieving the Avery Heart pad. She folded the top sheet over and sat the pad in front of her.

"Your man came to see me at Mount Vernon. We had lunch together, and he asked a lot of questions about my volunteer work there. I thought he was interested in being a volunteer, too. I had no idea he was investigating my ex-husband until he showed up at my home yesterday morning."

Nattie had spoken with Nathan the previous afternoon, when he virtually had surrendered the investigation of Jack Stout to her. *He must have taken it upon himself to turn his talent this way.*

"What happened?"

"That's precisely what I came here to explain," rebutted Shannon. "My ex-husband may be guilty of that robbery. I seriously doubt he is, but there's quite a lot about his business dealings I don't know, so I can't be sure. But whether or not he is guilty has no connection to me. We were in bankruptcy when we divorced, and then he went to prison, so I got nothing. *Nothing,*" she repeated louder, glaring at Nattie.

Nattie waited.

"Your man came to my home yesterday morning accusing me of hiding stolen art for Avery. He said you have evidence of my sister paying cash for my home in Alexandria."

"True." *Why in the world is Nathan throwing our evidence at our suspects?*

"And you think the cash came from an art auction in Philadelphia."

"Also true."

"Yes," she said as she withdrew a folded sheet of paper from her handbag. "Both of those facts are true. But those prints my sister sold in Philadelphia are ours. They've been in our family since the Civil War. Our great-great-great-great-grandfather was a reporter with the *Washington Gazette,* and those prints were drawings he made of Lincoln." She handed the pages over to Nattie.

"What's this?"

"That is a copy of my grandfather's will. As you can see, those pieces were listed in detail and left to my father in 1957."

Nattie looked at the document. It was as Shannon described. It was also stamped with a seal from the Union County, New Jersey, courthouse, so it would be easy to verify.

"May I have this?" asked Nattie.

"That's a copy," said Shannon. "It's yours."

"Thank you. Now, can I ask you about Avery's whereabouts?"

"You can ask, but I don't know where he is. He got released a month ago and visited our son one evening, but he doesn't want to see me any more than I want to see him."

"Does your son know where he is?"

"Possibly, but I'm sure you can contact him through his parole officer. I must ask you now to leave me and my son be. We have been embarrassed enough by this whole affair."

"I'm sure you understand that I will need to check this out. And since Avery is still a suspect, I still may need to ask you some questions, but if you give me a way to contact you discreetly, I'll make sure there will be no more surprise visits."

She leaned over the desk and scribbled her phone number on the empty pad of paper. "Please limit your calls to normal business hours." With that she turned and strode out of the room, her hair bouncing with every step.

CHAPTER 36

Kevin's Report on Rance Callahan

"WHAT WAS THAT ABOUT?" ASKED KEVIN as he plopped down in the seat across from Nattie's desk.

"Is she gone?"

"Oh, yeah. She bounced her hair outta here as fast as she bounced in. What did she want?"

"She wanted to explain about that artwork her sister sold in Philadelphia." She handed Kevin the will. "When you get the list from the auction house, we'll compare it to this. If it all checks out, then it's not part of the Holmes robbery."

After a quick glance at the page in his hand, Kevin said, "I don't think it's her anyway."

"We didn't really think she broke into the house. We thought she may have been an accomplice after the fact." Her voice trailed off when she noticed Kevin's forehead wrinkling as he listened. "That's not what you meant, is it?"

"Come look at this," he said, standing up. Waving his hand for her to follow, he went out of her office and sat at his own desk.

Nattie stood behind him as he typed on his keyboard.

"Check it out," he said, leaning back.

"What is that, Facebook?"

"Yeah."

"Why do I care about," she leaned closer to read the name, "Rance Callahan?"

He slid out of his chair. "Sit and see," he said.

"I'm busy, Kevin. Just tell me."

"Sit," he demanded. "You won't be disappointed."

She sat down and studied the page. The guy in the picture looked to be in his late thirties: baseball cap, sunglasses, no shirt, with the ocean behind him. The banner picture was of a golf foursome standing on a tee box.

Nattie moved the cursor over the "About" tab, but Kevin stopped her by putting his hand on top of hers. He pointed at the second man from the left in the golf photo. "Do you see who that is?"

She squinted. "Is that Presly Holmes?"

"It is." He leaned across her and typed Presly Holmes's name on the screen.

When Presly's banner picture appeared on the screen, it was the same foursome, but a different picture. In this picture, they were sitting around a table hoisting bottles of beer with a golf course in the background.

"Please tell me there's more to this than you discovered he's got golf buddies?"

Kevin leaned across her again and reloaded Rance Callahan's Facebook page. He pulled a chair around next to Nattie and sat. "I found Rance Callahan on Presly Holmes's Facebook page. He's in over half of the pictures of sports trips."

"Like I said, a golf buddy," said Nattie.

"Yeah, but here's the interesting thing. There are no pictures of him before 2010."

173

Nattie realized the implication immediately. "So they started traveling together after the burglary. Curious," said Nattie. She looked at Kevin. He was grinning. There was more he had to tell, and he was proud of it. "What else?" she asked.

"Until 2010 Rance Callahan was a private investigator out of Kingsport. That's when he dropped his license and moved to Chattanooga."

Nattie leaned closer.

Laughing, Kevin said, "That perked you up."

"Do we know why he dropped his license?"

"Apparently there was a complaint against him from one of his clients." He paused, waiting for Nattie's response.

"And . . . ," she prompted him.

"It was a houn' dog case, but instead of reporting back to the wife, he shook the husband down."

"And the wife reported him to the licensing board," guessed Nattie.

"The husband," said Kevin. "I guess the husband paid, but his wife found out anyway."

Nattie let all that digest a moment before saying, "Okay, Kevin. I get that this is a crooked PI, and now he and our crooked lawyer are golf buddies. What connection to this case are you seeing that I don't? I mean, I could see them pulling something crooked if they were buddy-buddy before, but then they'd hide their association, I'd think. This is just the opposite."

"They definitely had an association before, but it was just professional. Holmes represented Callahan in a divorce and then again in one of those houn' dog cases that got him sued. But it's Callahan's lifestyle change that jumps out at me."

"What do you mean?"

"Maybe they weren't golf buddies before the burglary because Callahan couldn't afford expensive golf trips."

Nattie's face lit up. "But now he can."

"Where's his money coming from, I wonder?"

"I'd say we'd better figure that out. Do you have an address for Mr. Callahan?"

He handed her a Mapquest page. "I figured the Alexandria trip would be off for now."

CHAPTER 37

Nattie Goes to Chattanooga to Rattle Rance's Cage

RANCE CALLAHAN REFERRED TO HIMSELF AS A BARTENDER on his Facebook page, but Kevin's search of financial records revealed that he was the bar's owner. The bar was located in an older industrial area of Chattanooga. It was aptly named The Saloon, as its décor was 1950s cowboy movie complete with a stand-up bar and brass footrest, round wooden tables and spindle chairs, and swinging shutters for an entrance.

It was almost two o'clock in the afternoon when Nattie walked in. She had hoped to miss whatever lunch crowd The Saloon drew, so when she arrived in Chattanooga she went to the Urban Stack Burger Lounge for a leisurely lunch of salad and bologna sliders. She was delighted that, other than Rance, there was only one person inside—a very large man standing at the far end of the bar with his left foot on the broken foot rail. The big man did not so much as glance at her when she entered.

Rance himself was sitting at one of the tables playing solitaire. When he saw Nattie, he made another play on his solitaire game, put the deck down, and leaned back on the back legs of his chair. "Now, what can I do for you, sweetheart?"

"Are you the owner?" she asked.

"Me and the bank," he said, chuckling.

"Mr. Callahan? Rance Callahan?"

"That's me." Setting his chair firmly back on four legs he frowned at her. "Who are you then?"

"My name is Nattie Moreland. I'm a PI from Bristol, and I'm here to ask you a few questions about your association with Mr. Presly Holmes."

"I'm not sure I know anyone by that name," he said. He turned toward the back of the room. "Hey, man, you need another V-8?"

The big guy shook his head no and waved his left hand in dismissal. He still did not look in their direction.

When Rance looked back, he picked up the deck of cards and resumed his solitaire game.

"Let me see if I can jog your memory," said Nattie. "Presly Holmes is a lawyer in Kingsport, where you were a PI yourself."

"I didn't do a lot of work for lawyers," he said offhandedly, still focusing on his game. "Mostly I did . . . ," he sneered up at Nattie, "domestic disputes."

"I'm aware of that, Mr. Callahan," said Nattie.

He snorted and began gathering up all the cards.

"I'm not here to talk about domestic dispute work."

Slamming the deck down, "So why are you here?"

She smiled. She was having exactly the effect she wanted. "I'm here about a robbery that took place at the Holmeses' home. Four and a half million in art."

He smirked as he shuffled the cards.

Nattie was standing to his left. When she placed her hands on the table and leaned forward, she was close enough to have backhanded him.

"What makes you think I know anything about any of that?" he asked as he set up another solitaire game.

She was ready for the question. Kevin's research had struck gold. "It seems that just before that robbery occurred, you rented a van from a U-Haul place in Greeneville, and two days later you returned it with 700 miles on it."

"So what?" he snarled, abandoning his game now.

"So, I don't know if you robbed that house or not, but I think you drove that van 350 miles from Greeneville and put the stolen articles in storage." She paused, stroking her chin philosophically. "So as long as I'm thinking out loud, let me add that none of that art has ever turned up, so it's still wherever you put it. Also, it was only a few months after that that you could suddenly afford to leave Kingsport and buy this fine establishment." She moved her left hand in a circular motion around the room. "That's why I believe you do know something about it. He paid you off with some of that insurance money, didn't he?"

He made a spitting noise.

"We'll find that art, Mr. Callahan. And when we do, you and Mr. Holmes will be looking at some serious time."

He shook his head slowly and forced a laugh. "You're blowing smoke, dolly. That's all it is: smoke."

"I'm going to find that art. With or without you, I'm going to find it. It will be easier on both of us if you tell me all about it now, but mark my words, Mr. Callahan, I'll find it. So, I'll ask again, what can you tell me about your association with Holmes?"

He once again tipped his chair back on two legs. "Here's what I got to say, dolly: You can take your threat and shove it."

He barely had time to enjoy his bravado because while the words were still in his mouth, Nattie bent over and cupped the dangling end of the left front chair leg, and then, without hesitation, she flipped it over. The effect was melodic as Rance's pitch changed an octave between the word "shove" and the word "it." His arms and legs flailed, grasping at nothing until he landed on his back.

The flailing continued as in his fury he tried to bounce up into a counterattack, but he struggled to gain a footing to push against. When he finally managed to get his upper body under control, he looked at Nattie and froze.

Nattie's Glock was pressed up against the middle of his forehead. "Stay there," she said, pushing him back with the muzzle.

When Rance leaned back, she pointed the gun at the big guy from the end of the bar who was moving toward her. "You, too," she ordered. "This is no concern of yours. Just stay over there."

The big guy raised both his hands and backed up to where he had been.

Turning her attention back to Rance Callahan, she said, "Last chance."

"I got nothing more to say," he growled.

"Okay." She lowered the gun to her side and stepped back. "I'll leave you to your business then. And if later you get curious about who Holmes is, you can look at your Facebook banner. Presly Holmes is the guy standing to your right."

CHAPTER 38

With Grandson Sam at Bays Mountain [Jack]

SAM AND I EACH CARRIED OUR OWN LUNCH BAGS from the Bays Mountain parking lot through the park.

We had begun having our excursions here to Bays Mountain when he was three. Back then I'd carry him half the time, and he'd walk half the time. But now that he's five he doesn't ask to be carried so much anymore.

We were headed to the aviary, but that meant passing by the wolf enclosure—and as expected, when it came into view, he turned around and lifted his hands. That's my signal, and I know what to do.

I carried him toward our spot, the bench across from the screech owl. That's where we would have our lunch: peanut butter and jelly sandwiches, baby carrots, apple slices, and juice boxes. Once we were past the wolves he began to squirm. When he was free again he ran to our bench and tossed his lunch bag on it so that it nearly stayed on top of the seat. He then began tending to his duties in front of the screech owl.

After retrieving Sam's lunch from behind the bench, I settled back to relax and enjoy being in one of my favorite places. I don't remember when my fondness for Bays Mountain began, but it was solidified during a sixth-grade field trip. We were studying the solar system so the planetarium was supposed to be the highlight of the trip, but for me it was the wolf enclosure.

An excursion to Bays Mountain has been an annual event for me since that sixth-grade trip. My mom would bring my sisters and me there for picnics in the summer. This was also where I brought Alice on our first real date. We checked out the wolves, which she tolerated, and walked slowly around the lake, which I found more than tolerable because the far side of the lake was where I kissed her the first time.

I'm not what you'd call smooth when it comes to the romance department, but kissing her was somehow easy. That thought brought an immediate laugh. Okay, that first kiss wasn't exactly easy. That's why we were all the way on the other side of the lake before I even tried. But once I tried it was easy. She made it easy.

I looked toward the lake. There were too many trees in the way to see the spot, but I could see it anyway. The memory was so enjoyable that I didn't see Sam running headlong toward me. I barely saw Sam launch himself knee first from the ground, but I was able to flinch just enough for Sam's knee to land in my midsection rather than my groin.

"Whatcha laughing at, Pop?" said Sam as he scrambled to his feet in my lap.

"I'm just enjoying being here with you, big guy," I told him. I did my best to hide that I was struggling to breathe.

He grabbed my face and turned my head so that we were eyeball to eyeball. "It's not nice to laugh at me," he told me. He sounded just like his mother, Cynthia, our oldest daughter.

"I wasn't laughing at you. I was thinking of your grandmother." That's what I told him. I didn't tell him what I was thinking, though. I didn't tell him that it took me halfway around the lake to kiss her the first time, but once I broke the ice I stopped to kiss her every ten feet the rest of the way around the lake. It was every ten feet because I didn't want to appear too eager.

Sam must have accepted that explanation of my laughter, because he hopped off my lap and returned to his heretofore unsuccessful attempts at getting the screech owl to screech. I had to hand it to him; he was persistent. This is the fourth time we had come here together, and he had yet to make the screech owl screech. He's not about to give up. He's like his grandmother that way.

I glanced down toward the wolf enclosure. It was midday, so I knew there'd be nothing to see. The wolves would be asleep and on the far side of the enclosure, but I looked anyway. Sure enough, the wolves were nowhere to be seen, but I did see Doug Hout's niece. She must have come after us because I didn't see her when we walked by, but then again Sam was fairly wrapped around my head as we passed by. *What's her name?* I wondered. I had met her a few times, but that had been long before Old Doug moved to Arizona.

She was taking pictures with a pretty fancy-looking camera. *Kayleigh,* I remembered. Her name was Kayleigh. I remembered that she was married, so her last name wasn't Hout, but I couldn't recall her last name. That's okay, though. I wasn't going to use her last name anyway if she was still there when Sam and I left.

"How ya doing, PeeWee?" I asked Sam.

He turned around slowly with a scowl on his face. "That's a bad word, Pop," he informed me.

I remembered that his mother was trying to correct his fascination with bathroom humor and body parts. "Pee-pee" was designated with "bad word" status, and I could only assume that "wee-wee" was, too. To his mind, "PeeWee" must have seemed like a double bad word. There was nowhere to hide.

"You're right, Sam. I didn't mean it bad, but I won't use that word again."

He eyed me carefully. I must have passed that test, too, because he nodded and climbed up on the seat next to me.

"How's it going with the owl?" I asked, thankful for a change of subject.

He shrugged.

"It's hard to get an owl to screech in the daytime, isn't it?"

He nodded yes.

"How are you trying to do it?" I asked.

"I make an owl face, but he won't look at me," said a sad Sam.

"He probably sees more than you think he's looking at."

Sam didn't look like he believed me.

"Show me your owl face," I requested.

He wiggled around to face me and opened his eyes wider while jutting his chin out.

"Well, that's the best owl face I've ever seen."

"I know," he said softly.

Screeeeeeeeeeeech!

It happened. That stupid bird screeched. It was a sound that rattled my fillings and made me jump, but Sam's face lit up like a Christmas tree.

"You did it," I told him.

He didn't hear me. His eyes were locked on the owl. There was no room for anything else.

After a few minutes he stood up on the bench and put his arm around my shoulder.

"Hungry?"

He nodded yes.

"Do you want to eat here or down by the lake?"

"McDonald's."

Of course, he was right. You can't just eat a regular old bag lunch after a victory like that. "Okay," I said, "let's go get some Happy Meals."

Maybe Sam didn't remember the wolves. They were on the far side of the enclosure fast asleep, but still, he had remembered them on the

183

way in. Now he was running ahead of me. There's nothing like making a screech owl screech to make a man feel like a man.

"Slow down, big guy," I called out to him.

He dropped to one knee and waited for me about fifteen feet from where Kayleigh stood, still holding her camera. She was no longer alone; a couple was talking to her. She seemed to be explaining something as she pointed to the other side of the enclosure. I didn't really pay attention to the guy—partly because his back was to me, but mostly because the girl looked like a Brazilian swimsuit model.

I looked away from her just in time to keep from stepping on Sam, who was trying to get an ant to climb up on a stick he was holding.

"Mr. Stout?"

The voice was familiar, but I didn't immediately realize who was attached to it.

"It's me, Kevin Johnson," he said as he turned fully around toward me. "We met at my parents' house one Sunday afternoon a while ago."

It was the detective's brother. "Of course, Kevin. I remember. How are you?"

I didn't think it was the right time to ask what I wanted to ask: "Caught the thief yet?"

Sam seemed content, so I walked ten yards past him.

Kevin and I shook hands. His hands weren't calloused like the hands I usually shake, but his grip was firm enough.

"Nattie and I met Mr. Stout at my mom's that Sunday when you couldn't go to lunch with us," he explained to the swimsuit model.

"Mr. Stout," she said, extending her hand, "I'm Knox."

"Please," I told them. "Everyone calls me Jack."

"And this is, ahhh—" Kevin looked squeamishly at Kayleigh. "I'm sorry."

"This is Kayleigh," said Knox. "She's giving us the tour of the wolves."

I tipped my head at Kayleigh. "I think we've met before. You're Doug Hout's niece, aren't you?"

"I am," she said. "Are you a friend of Uncle Doug's?"

"We worked together at the city," I answered, "back before he moved."

"Who's your friend?" asked Kevin as Sam began walking carefully back toward the aviary.

"That's my grandson, Sam. We come here whenever he visits. He's been trying to get the screech owl to screech, and today he did. We're going for Happy Meals to celebrate."

"What's he doing now?" asked Knox.

We all watched as he continued, concentrating on the stick he held out away from his body.

"I'm guessing he's got a bug on that stick and he's gonna give it to the owl," said Kevin.

"That sounds about right," I agreed.

Sam stopped suddenly, brought the stick closer to his face, and studied it.

As we watched Sam throw the stick and sulk back toward us, Kevin added, "I'm guessing the bug's gone now."

He was still a little unhappy when he got to me, so he didn't resist me picking him up. I held him on the hip next to Knox.

"We heard you made the owl screech," Knox told Sam.

Suddenly he wasn't unhappy anymore. "We're going to Mc-Donald's."

"We know," Knox said. "Your granddad told us."

Sam beamed.

"We'd better get on with it," I said. "It was good to see you all. Enjoy the wolves."

As we walked away Sam informed me, "She's pretty."

"I noticed that, too."

185

CHAPTER 39

Stone Fort Inn

NATTIE LEFT THE SALOON AND DROVE IMMEDIATELY downtown to check into her hotel, the Stone Fort Inn, in downtown Chattanooga.

At four o'clock she went to the bar. It was dark and pretty well deserted. Sitting at the end of the bar closest to the door was a man in a dark blue suit that looked like he had run a marathon in it. He was attempting to schmooze someone on his cell phone. *You're not coming off like you think you're coming off,* Nattie wanted to tell him.

The only other patrons were a couple sitting at a table toward the back. Unlike the man at the bar, they were taking great pains to not be heard. The man was a well-dressed and distinguished-looking man whom Nattie took to be about Lionel's age. He looked like Lionel. The woman looked nothing like Knox, but Nattie gauged her age to be close to Knox's.

Nattie settled in at the far end of the bar and was immediately attended to by the bartender, a very clean-cut twenty-something male. His name tag identified him as George.

"Tonic and lime," said Nattie.

"Gin or vodka?" asked George.

"Just tonic and lime. Thanks."

By the time her drink came, she had fired up the Kindle app on her phone and resumed reading *David and Goliath* by Malcolm Gladwell. Her drink was half gone when the noise in the room suddenly stopped.

The first person Nattie saw when she looked up was George behind the bar. He was stark still and staring at the doorway.

Nattie swiveled to see what the attraction was. In the doorway stood a huge man. His thinning hair was pulled back in a ponytail, and the way he folded his arms accentuated how muscular his forearms were. He was scanning the room looking for someone. Nattie recognized the man who earlier had been sitting in Rance Callahan's saloon. When he spotted Nattie he unfolded his arms and crossed the room toward her.

"Well," Nattie said as the huge man settled in next to her, "did he bite?"

The man snorted. "Are you kidding? Did he buy it that you would have shot him? I bought that you would have shot me, and I was in on it."

Nattie's smile had a touch of embarrassment.

"I didn't expect you to kick him over like that."

"What did you learn, Beau?"

"One thing I know for sure is I'm never gonna say 'shove it' to you."

"Can I get you anything to drink?" asked George, who had waited longer to approach Beau than he had Nattie.

Beau looked down at Nattie's glass. "I'll have one of those."

"It's not a real drink," said George.

"Is it . . . wet?"

George hesitated like he suspected it was a trick question. "Of course."

"It'll do then. Thanks." When George was out of hearing distance Beau leaned toward Nattie. "He'll make the call. First he's gonna check me out, but that'll be fine. He's gonna find out I was a counselor in New Orleans and lost my license. That should qualify me as one of the bad guys." He looked away as he spoke.

George, who was walking back with the drink, quickened his step.

Nattie placed her right hand on his left forearm, which was leaning against the edge of the bar. Beau didn't look, but as soon as she touched him, his shoulders relaxed slightly.

"Thanks, George," said Beau when his drink was delivered. "Good man."

Beau took a long drag on his tonic before turning to Nattie. "The kid's right. That's not a real drink."

"But it is wet," returned Nattie. "So now we wait."

"Now we wait."

"You going to show me around Chattanooga while we wait?"

At five-thirty they walked from the Stone Fort Inn to Alleia's.

"I thought about taking you to Big River," Beau told her. "They have the best meatloaf since my memaw's."

"We could go there."

"Maybe next time," he said as he swung the giant wood door open. "This always reminds me of a castle door. Wait 'til you see the fireplace."

"Two?" asked the hostess.

"Please," answered Beau. "And we'd like a good view of the fire-place."

The hostess, a chunky thirty-something woman with short curly hair, smiled and said, "You've been here before."

"I have."

"I thought I recognized you. Is this your wife?"

Beau looked at Nattie and grinned, "She wishes."

The hostess blushed slightly and glanced at Nattie apologetically.

With a flip of her hand Nattie said, "What can I say? He's hard to catch."

The hostess leaned toward Nattie. "Have you tried meatloaf? That's how I got mine."

"That," said Nattie, with a tip of her head toward the hostess, "was going to be my very next strategy."

On Beau's recommendation Nattie ordered the grilled romaine salad and followed that with pumpkin ravioli and braised pork. Beau had the same.

"Save room for dessert," he told her.

When they left, people were waiting to get in.

The Hot Chocolatier was another short walk for them. On the way, Beau's cell phone rang.

"Yeah."

Pause. He looked at Nattie and nodded yes.

"I don't know if I can do that," said Beau, frowning at Nattie. Then suddenly he pulled his head back and scowled at his phone. "The sleaze just hung up on me."

"What's up?" asked Nattie.

"He said he's willing to go get the stuff, but he wants five hundred bucks up front."

"That's what 'I don't know if I can do that' meant?" questioned Nattie.

"Yeah," answered Beau. "And that's when he said, 'Call me when you figger it out, pony boy.'" Beau bared his teeth. "That skidmark called me 'pony boy.'"

"Five hundred dollars," repeated Nattie more out loud than to Beau. "You don't think he's going to get it himself, do you?"

"Yeah, I do," answered Beau. "Looking at that saloon of his I'd say he couldn't hire someone to get it."

"But don't you think he'd be worried that I'd follow him?"

"He should, but he's not exactly a master criminal. Besides, after the way you manhandled him, I'll bet that outmaneuvering you is a point of pride for him."

She raised her eyebrows and gave her head a ditzy shake. "Men and their points of pride."

Beau pointed at her head. "Cute," he said. "Now, what do you want to do about that $500?"

Nattie took a slow breath. "How much did you agree to pay him for the goods?"

"Ten cents on the dollar. He said they had $350,000 worth of art and stuff. That's what he called it: 'stuff.'"

"So he wants $500 up front against a $35,000 payoff?" Nattie flipped her hands over. "I think we have to pay it. We don't want him to think you can't get the $35,000, do we?"

"Nope, but do you have $500 to front him?"

"Not on me, but I can have it after the bank opens in the morning. I'll have Kevin put it on my debit card first thing."

"Are you sure?"

"It's our plan," she said. "We have to see it all the way out."

Beau nodded his agreement.

"Go ahead. Make the call, pony boy."

"'Pony boy'?" he repeated in a higher-than-normal pitch. "You're kinda bold insulting me like that right after telling me you've got your debit card on ya and you're buying dessert."

CHAPTER 40

Breakfast at the Bluegrass Grill

THEY HAD PLANNED ON EATING BREAKFAST at Aretha Franken-stein's. Beau had promised her better pancakes than her mother made.

The plans got altered, however, when Rance said he needed the money by dawn. Beau told him he'd have the money after the banks opened, and they agreed to meet at Rance's bar around nine-thirty. That meant an early breakfast within walking distance of Nattie's hotel.

"You'll love the Bluegrass Grill," Beau told her the night before. "They open at six-thirty, and breakfast is their specialty."

Beau was already seated when Nattie arrived at seven-ten. He was reading the paper and sipping black coffee. The waitress, a slender thirty-something with freckles and auburn hair pulled back in a pony-tail, led Nattie to the table. She mumbled something about getting Nattie coffee as she left.

The thought to tell her to make it decaf came too late to matter.

"How'd ya sleep?" asked Beau.

"Okay," said Nattie as she sat down and picked up the menu lying on the table. "Nothing sleeps like my own bed, but it was a nice room with a good mattress."

Beau patted his torso. "If a good mattress matters to a lightweight like you, imagine what it means to a wide-body like me."

Nattie pointed at his hands working his midsection. "Are you still trying to digest that dessert from last night?"

He grinned. At the Hot Chocolatier he had ordered "the biggest dessert ya got." It was some sort of brownie topped with a chocolate mousse and decorated with dark chocolate pieces and strawberries. He didn't even offer to share. Nattie had a cocoa and a shortbread cookie.

"I'm okay," said Beau. "I'm ready for a big breakfast, too. I recommend the omelets, but everything is good."

The waitress, Connie, came back with a pot of coffee and a mug. "Decaf, right? He said you'd want decaf."

"Yes. Please."

"Know what you want?"

Beau ordered a Mexican salsa omelet with jalapeno bacon and a side of grits. Nattie chose the portobello mushroom hash with Swiss cheese. They sipped their coffees and ate their meals in the kind of silence that often precedes an anxiously waited-for moment. Neither wanted to upset the delicate balance between hopeful anticipation and worrisome second thoughts.

After Connie had cleared their dishes and refilled their cups Nattie looked at her watch and broke the silence. "It's quarter to eight. We probably won't hear from Kevin for another half hour."

"I told your cowboy that I wouldn't have his money until after nine, so we're okay on time," said Beau.

"Is this going to work?" she asked out loud.

"Of course."

Nattie sighed.

"He's not going to skip town with five hundred dollars," said Beau. "He's got everything he owns tied up in that bar, and it ain't cutting it. He needs this score."

"I know you're right," Nattie said. "Waiting around for something to happen is just not my best skill."

"Really?" He sounded surprised. "Don't you have to do a lot of surveillance jobs?"

"I do."

"Well, how do you pass the time when you're watching some guy's door all night?"

"I make top-ten lists."

"There you go, Nattie. Let's make a top-ten list. How about top ten jazz musicians?"

"I don't know any jazz musicians. How about an all-star Chicago Cubs team?"

"That's baseball, right?" Beau asked with a straight face.

"Nice hair," she told him.

When he was done snickering heartily he told her, "You know, Nathan told me what that meant."

"I don't know what you mean," she said in her sweetest voice.

He leaned closer. "I know that when you say 'nice hair' out loud to yourself, you add, 'considering how far your head is up your—'"

"Can I get you anything else?" asked Connie as she sat the bill on the edge of the table.

"We're good, thank you," said Nattie.

When Connie left with Nattie's credit card, Beau asked, "What's a top-ten list we could both get into? I know. How about the top ten attractions here in Chattanooga? We've got the aquarium, Rock City, and the Lookouts."

"I know as much about Chattanooga as I do about jazz musicians," said Nattie. "Let's make it Bristol."

"Rhythm & Roots," offered Beau, "and the racetrack."

"South Holston Lake and the Barter Theater in Abingdon," countered Nattie.

"Johnson City has the Cardinals. What else?"

"The Hands-On Museum."

"We've got the Creative Discovery Museum," bragged Beau.

"Kingsport's got Bays Mountain and Funfest," countered Nattie, then she suddenly sat upright and reached for her phone. She touched the screen a couple of times and then looked up. "Kevin says the money's in the bank. As soon as I sign the check, we can go get the cash."

"Game time," smiled Beau.

CHAPTER 41

Presly Is Arrested

[Two days later.]

FBI AGENT MOE ROSS WAS STANDING NEXT TO NATTIE when her phone rang. It was just before one o'clock. They were standing in front of the Nutty Java II on the corner of Broad and Market Streets in Kingsport, a half block from Presly Holmes's office. One member of Moe's squad, a former basketball player named Cynthia Horton Hale, stood next to Moe on the sidewalk. Most of her squad, three men, were inside having coffee. Federation Fidelity had called in the FBI after Nattie had informed Federation of her plan. She would have used Kingsport PD, but since it wasn't her money, it wasn't her call.

The call they were waiting for was to come from Karen Rohr, an FBI agent in Chattanooga. Agent Rohr specialized in profiling and psychological interrogation. When Nattie asked how sure they were that Rance Callahan would roll over on Presly Holmes, Moe said, "Karen Rohr may look like a nice lady when she drives up in her lime-green Volkswagen wearing Birkenstocks and a floral dress, but nobody tends to details like Rohr. Your buddy Callahan is going to roll over. I guarantee it."

Nattie glanced through the window. Agent Ross's crew was sitting in a conversational circle of upholstered furniture just inside the door. They seemed fairly relaxed while keeping a constant eye open for Ross's signal. If she gave a thumbs-up, their coffee break was over. At the bar on the right side of the café, Nattie's crew sat perched on bar chairs. Kevin and Knox watched the FBI agents like star-struck teenagers. Nathan and the owner, Carl Matherly, were in their own world laughing about whatever was being said.

Nattie had negotiated for her and Knox to be allowed close proximity to the Holmes arrest. She wanted to be part of the arrest team, but that wasn't allowed, so she settled on being nearby when they brought him out. Nathan and Kevin were there because they each felt it was their responsibility as men to be there. Kevin was also hoping to get official FBI windbreakers.

"I've got some of those ball caps we give to kids in my trunk," Agent Ross told Nattie. "Remind me when we get this wrapped up," she added to Cynthia.

It was the third phone call Agent Ross had received while they waited. Her phone face told Nattie nothing. She was still listening when she slowly turned toward the window. She didn't nod or mouth anything. All she did was make eye contact with her team, and they immediately swung into gear.

The first two men out of the door trotted around to the alley behind the row of buildings. The other agent followed closely by Moe and Cynthia as they made their way down the sidewalk toward Presly's office. They moved briskly, ignoring the stares that came from nearly everyone who saw them.

Nattie and Knox followed behind. None of them spoke or even glanced to the left or right until they arrived at Presly's building, where Agent Byron turned and pointed at them. "Here's where you stop," she told them. She looked across the street to where Nathan and Kevin were standing and added, "Make sure those two stay over there."

Although it seemed much longer to them, it only took twenty minutes for the FBI to bring out Presly Holmes. He was handcuffed and escorted by an agent on either side of him. He looked smug, like he was enjoying the attention, as they escorted him toward their black Suburban with the dark-tinted windows. He grinned and tipped his head toward Cynthia, the agent who was on his left.

He's going to tick her off, thought Nattie as she watched.

Before he said whatever he was going to say, Presly noticed Nattie and Knox watching him. They had chosen to sit where they knew he'd be sure to look, on the trunk of his canary-yellow Jaguar. Nattie and Presly were ten feet apart and staring directly at each other.

"Git your ass off of that car," he threatened, lunging toward them.

The agents, who had his arms, quickly pulled him backward and upright.

"I don't think he remembers you," said Knox, making a point of squirming back and forth across the Jaguar.

Nattie kept her eyes locked on the tall man while he struggled against the constraint of the two FBI agents. When he finally settled down to an angry scowl, she said, "We just wanted to come down and see you off."

"Shove it," he sneered.

Nattie hopped off the car and took another two quick steps before kicking her foot up between his legs as the agents held him in place. She pulled up short rather than connect the kick, but he flinched away nonetheless. With his hands handcuffed behind him and his arms held in place by his escorts, the move had the effect of taking his legs out from underneath him. He seemed to hover awkwardly for a moment before falling on his unprotected face.

"Awww," says Knox, "that looked like it hurt."

Nattie felt first delighted and then guilty quickly thereafter. She took a step toward helping him, but the agents were already on it.

"Ugly bitch," he snarled. His nose was bleeding.

Nattie placed the fingertips of her right hand lightly on her chest and in a breathy voice said, "Gasp."

CHAPTER 42

His Good Word [Jack]

I'VE BEEN A MEMBER OF THE HOLSTON VALLEY RURITAN CLUB for five years. We're a service club. We do quite a bit of projects for local youth: college scholarships, ball fields, and athletic tournaments. We've also helped out with several Red Cross disasters. Our fundraisers include helping out with all sorts of local events. My favorite event is our own soup dinner. For six bucks our patrons can have their choice of any three of twenty-plus soups all lined up in Crock-Pots along one wall, and they can go through the line as many times as they want, or can. The dessert table has just as many selections. We generally raise about four thousand dollars for college scholarships.

Alice made a corn chowder and two meringue pies, chocolate and butterscotch. The butterscotch was supposed to stay home for me, but what was I going to say when she took it in? She worked the drink table from eleven to one while I had ladle duty behind three types of chili: spicy, meatless, and beanless.

My relief came early, so naturally I scoped out the dessert table. That butterscotch pie she brought was supposed to be mine, and I intended to have at least one piece of it. Alice's relief wasn't there yet, which would have been fine because I could go ahead and have a piece of butterscotch pie while I waited for her. It would have been fine, that is, if there had been any butterscotch pie left.

I took a consolation whoopie pie. It was an appetizer. It was also gone in three bites. I figured I'd have another after lunch.

As I pushed the last of the three bites into my mouth, I had to turn away from where Alice was watching from the drink table. If I was reading Alice's facial expression correctly, and I was, I was setting a bad example of table manners for the kiddos trying to get their own appetizers.

When I turned I was facing the front door, allowing me to catch sight of something that took all the sweet out of that last bite. Let me add that a bite that size is much harder to get down when the sweet is gone.

What I saw was the private investigator Nattie and her brother, Kevin. They were at the cashier with their backs to me, so they hadn't seen me yet. It was possible, I suppose, that they weren't here to see me, but it didn't feel like it. My stomach was knotted, and a third of a whoopie pie was parked halfway down my throat.

I scrambled back to the drink table and downed a cup of sweet tea in a couple of gulps. This brought an I'm-watching-you, schoolteacher look from Alice. Once I could breathe again, I turned back toward the front to check on Nattie and her brother. They were headed my way. At least she was smiling. At least I could breathe again.

"Mr. Stout," said Nattie as she came closer, "your wife told us you'd be here."

I looked at Alice. She was as close to Nattie as I was, but she was busying herself with filling empty cups with ice while she pretended not to hear.

"I've got some good news for you," said Nattie. "Can we talk over there a minute?" She pointed to the back corner where we could talk alone.

"I would have called you last night," Nattie began once we were out of earshot of others, "but I wanted to tell you this in person."

It was feeling like good news. Nattie's face was illuminated with her smile. It was the first time I noticed how pretty her eyes were. "What?" I said, sounding like Goofy.

"We arrested someone yesterday afternoon."

"It's over?" I questioned, not sure why I wasn't more elated.

"It's over," she assured me.

"It's over?" asked Alice as she joined us. She sounded elated but wanting it validated.

"It's over," confirmed Kevin.

I couldn't help but laugh. "It's over. It's over," I chanted as I bear-hugged Nattie first, as she was standing next to me, then Alice.

"It's not over," said Kenneth, another Ruritan member, who had come closer when he saw all the commotion. "I don't know what he's telling you folks," he said to Nattie and Kevin, "but we're open until seven. We've got lots of soup, and more is on the way."

Alice asked them to join us for lunch. We each got three bowls of soup, two of which were the bear vegetable and the sausage corn chowder, which was not the same soup as Alice brought. Everyone else got the shrimp gumbo, but I got the chicken and dumplin's.

Nattie sat across from me. Kevin sat across from Alice.

"So," said Alice, "fill me in on the details."

"We can't tell you much," said Nattie in a quiet voice, "but like I told your husband, we arrested someone yesterday. It's still an ongoing investigation, so we can't say more than that."

"But Jack's in the clear, right?" Alice asked. Under the table she was holding my hand.

"It's not official yet, but yes, I'd say he's in the clear," said Nattie.

Alice squeezed my hand.

"What did you think 'It's over' meant a minute ago?" I asked.

She squeezed my hand again. "I knew what I hoped it meant, but I wanted to be sure."

"Let's talk about something else," suggested Kevin.

"What do you have in mind?" I asked.

"How about Bays Mountain? Did your grandson get his Happy Meal?"

All eyes turned to me. We hadn't told Alice that we had thrown away the bag lunches she sent with us. "You remember," I said to Alice, "it was the time when Sam made the screech owl screech. I took him out for Happy Meals to celebrate."

Alice raised her right eyebrow, which didn't necessarily mean I was in trouble. It just meant she wanted me to squirm.

"It was a special occasion," I said with the required amount of squirm.

"What were you doing on Bays Mountain?" Nattie asked Kevin.

"Knox took me. She wanted to show me the wolves. We ran into that woman she met when she was with you."

"What woman?" asked Nattie.

"The lawyer's secretary," answered Kevin.

"Really," I said. "Kayleigh is Holmes's secretary."

"That's what Knox told me," responded Kevin. "And she really knows a lot about wolves. She's an expert."

"I didn't know that," I said.

"I didn't either," agreed Nattie. "I know she has a huge collection of wolf photos at her office, but I didn't know she was an expert." Then she looked at me and asked, "How do you know her?"

"I know her uncle. He was the building inspector in Kingsport before me."

"Mr. Hout?" said Nattie. It surprised me that she knew him.

"You know Doug?" I questioned.

"I met him once when I went to Betty's to find you. He seems like a nice man, and he sure respects you."

I didn't know what to say to that. Alice squeezed my hand once more and let go, and I went back to eating soup.

Kevin finished his third bowl as I finished my second.

"How was that chicken and dumplin's?" asked Kevin.

My mouth was full of bear soup when he asked, so all I could do was moan.

"That means he likes it," translated Alice.

"Good enough for me," announced Kevin as he hopped up and headed back to the soup buffet.

Kevin returned just as I finished my third bowl of soup. "Anyone want dessert?" I asked.

"Thanks, but no," said Nattie, who was keeping pace—a very slow pace—with Alice.

I knew Alice was a no on dessert. I asked Kevin, "Whoopie pie?"

He gave me a smile and a nod.

Kenneth's wife, Mary Jane, was tending the dessert table when I got there. "Those are for kids," she told me with a twinkle in her eyes while I helped myself to two more whoopee pies.

"Good thing we're all kids," she added when she saw me hesitate.

Alice eyed my choice with furrowed brow when I returned with the pies. "I'm celebrating," I explained.

"So that's a whoopie pie," said Nattie.

"You were thinking of whoopee cushions, weren't you?" asked Alice as she moved my dessert across the table to Nattie.

I tried to hide my shock, but honestly I don't know how well I did. Mostly I was dumbfounded. And then Suzi Lawson leaned over my right shoulder and placed a slice of butterscotch pie in front of me.

"I was supposed to give you this when you came to the dessert table," Suzi told me, "but I was gone when you came by. Mary Jane told me what she said to you, so I knew I had missed you. It's from Alice." She patted me on the shoulder. "Better late than never, right?"

Right, I thought, but I didn't speak because my mouth was full.

"Thanks, Suzi," said Alice.

My pie was gone before Nattie had taken a second bite of my—I mean, her—whoopie pie. I tried not to be too obvious as I watched her eat it. Then I realized that she looked a lot like one of the actresses from the *Heroes* television show.

"I have a question," announced Nattie.

"Shoot," I told her. It took her a moment to figure out what I meant.

"A friend from Chattanooga and I were talking the other day about the top ten attractions around Bristol and I mentioned Kingsport's Funfest, but I'm not really sure what it is. I've seen the signs for years, but I've never been."

"It's really a whole week of activities," explained Alice. "There's a scavenger hunt, a Mardi Gras–type parade, and there's always a big concert. It's Chicago this year."

"Really," piped in Kevin. "We love the old stuff." To Nattie he said, "We should go."

CHAPTER 43

The Check

"IT'S EXPENSIVE," EXPLAINED NATHAN. He was referring to the cigar in his mouth. He was referring to the cigar Nattie had just asked him to throw out.

"I don't care how much it costs. It stinks." Nattie scanned around her waiting room. Seeing Kevin behind his desk she pointed, "Remember that time when you were in the sixth grade and you ate all that?"

"Why do you want to bring that up?" whined Kevin.

Nattie explained to Nathan, "He went to a sleepover the night before we drove to the Outer Banks for vacation. It rained, so we had to keep all the windows closed." She looked back at Kevin. "Lionel kept growling, 'Is someone sick?'"

"Air biscuits," explained Kevin.

"Radioactive air biscuits," amplified Nattie before turning to point at Nathan's cigar, "and that's worse."

Nathan handed her an envelope. While keeping the cigar in his mouth he mumbled, "Maybe that will help."

The return address read Federation Fidelity. It was addressed to Nathan Moreland and had not yet been opened.

"Is this what I think it is?"

Removing the cigar, "I'd say it's an unopened envelope."

"Seriously, Nathan, is this the check?"

Kevin came over to them. *"The* check?"

"Open it," said Nathan.

"Yeah, Sarge, open it," added Kevin.

She held it up to the overhead light before tearing one end off the envelope. Then she blew into it and slid out the contents, which consisted of a letter and a business check. The business check was attached to a stub and folded over so that it had to be folded open to be seen. Kevin and Nathan huddled on either side of her, watching intently as she folded back the stub.

"Five!" shouted Nathan, throwing his head back. He removed the cigar from his mouth and roared, "Five hundred thousand dollars. Five . . . hundred . . . thousand . . . dollars."

Nattie and Kevin looked at each other, not knowing what to say.

Kevin backed up.

Nattie cleared her throat: "Nathan."

He was too busy doing his version of Riverdance to hear her.

"Nathan," she repeated louder and much more urgently.

He froze.

"You need to look at this check again."

He took a step closer, grabbed the check, and retreated to where he had been standing. He did all this without taking his eyes off Nattie. He stood, breathing heavily and holding the check at his side in his left hand. The cigar in his right hand was held below his waist as well.

Nattie pointed. "Look at the check."

He looked down at the check. His head moved slowly back and forth as he studied the numbers. Then, scowling, he lifted the cigar as if to throw it. He scanned the room frantically before dashing madly for the door, where he threw the cigar across the parking lot.

"There's an explanation," said Nattie calmly.

Spinning back around, Nathan held his left fist out toward her. The check crumpled in his grip. "Five thousand dollars. Those lying bastards think they can cheat me. I've got a contract."

"That's right, you have a contract, so you have protection. It's probably just a mistake. Let's get to the bottom of it before we get all excited."

"'Before we get all excited,'" he repeated as he stomped. Pounding on the check with his right hand he said, "This is supposed to be four hundred thousand dollars."

She held up her hands. "I know. But there's nothing to be gained by getting upset before we find out what's up." Turning to Kevin, who was standing behind his desk, she instructed, "Get them on the phone."

She looked at the letter. It was signed by an Edward Embree. Taking the letter over to Kevin she said, "I want to talk to this guy.

"And you," she said to Nathan. "You go figure out how to calm down. I'll let you know when I know something. Until then I don't want you here wearing out my carpet."

It was ten-thirty when Nathan left Nattie's office. At eleven-fifteen she called him to say that she had made contact with Edward Embree and was waiting for a fax. Nathan was not, she told him, under any circumstances, to return until two-thirty.

At precisely two-fifteen, Nathan entered the office with a large box from Blackbird Bakery, announcing, "I know I'm early, but I brought upside-down cupcakes."

From the doorway Nathan could see Nattie sitting at Kevin's desk. Knox was standing behind her, and Kevin behind them both. All three, who had been looking at something on Kevin's desk, looked up at the same time.

"The fax will be coming soon," said Nattie.

"I'll make coffee," said Kevin.

"Upside-down cupcakes?" asked Knox.

Nathan handed the box to Knox. "Chocolate, coconut, and lemon. From Blackbird Bakery." He circled around them and asked, "What's the story?"

Standing up, Nattie placed her left hand on his chest and pointed toward her office with her right. "Go. All of you, go. The fax will come any moment, and when it's all done coming through we'll look at it in my office. So let's all go in my office now and eat donuts."

"It's not donuts, it's—" began Nathan.

"Come on," Nattie repeated with a gentle shove against Nathan's chest.

Knox, carrying the Blackbird Bakery box, gathered small paper plates, napkins, and a knife from the cabinets behind Kevin's desk and followed Nattie. Kevin, who was making the coffee, waited for the dripping to stop before joining them in Nattie's office.

Nathan paced along the back wall as Knox cut the three cupcakes into quarters. Then, while Knox passed out the portions to everyone, Kevin poured the coffee.

Nattie sat patiently amid the activities, leaning against the front of her desk listening for the fax machine. When she heard the machine come on, she stood up, alerting everyone else to the sound. They all stared at the door and listened to the hum. When the machine went quiet again, Nattie looked at Kevin and nodded her head once.

A minute later Kevin returned to the room with the fax. "It's a list," he said, handing the pages to Nattie, who had returned to her seat behind the desk.

Nattie glanced over the list as Nathan hovered over her. It was a list of the items recovered when Rance Callahan was arrested.

"How are we supposed to know if that's complete?" snarled Nathan.

"Hold on," Nattie told him as she searched through her file drawer. She placed a file on the center of her desk and opened it. It only took a moment to find the document she was looking for. "This is the list we got from Presly Holmes," she said, handing it to Kevin. "Read it."

Kevin began doing as he was told.

"Read it out loud," she corrected him. "One item at a time."

"Small Picasso," read Kevin.

"Check," said Nattie.

"Two-foot-by-two-foot oil still life by A. Morris," he read.

"Check."

"One-foot-by-one-foot portrait of young girl by J. Hensley," he read.

Nattie nodded, "Next."

"Three Gutenberg Bible pages."

"Next."

"Landscape in pastels by E. Rymer."

"Next."

"One-foot-by-three-foot ocean scene by D. Buck."

Nattie nodded.

"Three-foot-by-five-foot oil painting of lions by A. Cullop."

"Next."

"Bust of Socrates by C. Tidman."

Kevin continued to read until he had read all four pages. When he was done, all eyes focused on Nattie.

"Well?" asked Nathan impatiently.

Nattie looked up from her list. "There's nothing missing from this list."

"You're kidding," snapped Nathan.

"No, the lists are identical." She offered the list to Nathan.

He didn't take it. Instead he asked, "But they changed all the values, right?"

"It doesn't look that way."

Nathan turned for the door.

"Nathan, where are you going?" Nattie's voice cracked.

"I don't know," he answered without stopping.

"How about you, Sis?" asked Kevin once Nathan had cleared the door. "Where are you going with this now?"

"I don't know, either," she said, still staring at the door.

CHAPTER 44

Back to Go

NATTIE DID A QUICK SURVEY OF THE CUPCAKE PLATES. Hers was still full, as was Nathan's. Knox had eaten one of her portions, and Kevin's plate, as expected, was empty. "How are they?" she asked, biting the lemon piece in two.

"Great," answered Kevin. "You get more icing when they're upside down."

Nattie put the other half of lemon cupcake back on the plate and slid it across the desk toward Kevin. "It's good, but I'm too wired to eat anything sweet." She took a drag from her coffee cup.

"Before you drink that coffee and get even more wired than you already are, can I make a suggestion?" asked Knox.

Nattie looked at her and nodded.

"I don't know if it's the same, but when I'm writing a song and I get stuck, sometimes I need to get away from it. You know, like go away and do something completely different."

"That's great advice, Knox. Thank you," responded Nattie. "I don't think I'm stuck so much as we thought we had it solved and now we don't. It's 'back to Go' time."

Knox's shoulders slumped forward as she looked down. "That's okay," she said sheepishly.

"But I'll tell you what," continued Nattie. "I am a little fried right now, so I want you to do me a favor."

Knox looked up.

"If it ever looks to you like I'm stuck or burned out or frustrated, I want you to just tell me, 'It's time.'" She reached her hand across the desk toward Knox. "I'll know what you mean, and I'll call it quits for the day."

Knox lightly squeezed Nattie's hand and smiled.

"What's up?" asked Kevin, looking up from Nattie's empty plate.

"We're going back to 'Go,'" explained Knox.

He did a double take. "Back to Go"—as in, back to the beginning of a Monopoly board—was an expression he had heard Nattie use many times. Actually, it was an expression he had heard their grandfather, the Wolf, use many times. So he knew exactly what it meant. What had surprised him was hearing it come from Knox's lips.

"Do you think the insurance company is cheating us?" asked Knox.

Nattie placed the two lists next to each other and slid them toward Knox. "If they are, I don't see it."

Knox leaned over to study the lists, both first pages, then both seconds, and so on. When she had worked her way through all four pages of each, she looked up at Nattie, frowning.

"What is it?" inquired Nattie.

Sliding both lists back to Nattie, "I don't see any coins."

Nattie picked up the list from Federation Fidelity and ran her finger slowly down each page. "No coins," she muttered to herself, picking up the Presly Holmes list. When she finally put that list down she announced, "No coins."

"'No coins,'" repeated Kevin. "What does that mean?"

"It means there is more to this than we thought," stated Nattie.

"But that Holmes pig is still guilty, isn't he?" asked Knox.

"I think we can say for sure he's guilty of stealing what we recovered so far," began Nattie, "but there's a lot of money tied up somewhere else. If we didn't recover any coins in Chattanooga, then it makes sense for no coins to show up on the Federation list, but why are the coins missing from the Holmes list?"

"Holmes is guilty. We know that, right?" asked Knox.

Nattie nodded yes.

"Well, he could be guilty of more than we thought, right?" continued Knox.

"He's definitely guilty of more than we thought," agreed Nattie. "But we got everything Rance took from their house. I'm sure of that. It's not too hard to see how Holmes would benefit from keeping something from his partner."

"It's got to be Holmes," said Knox. "If not Holmes, then who?"

"You don't think it could be Mr. Stout, do you?" asked Kevin tentatively.

"I don't want to," admitted Nattie, "but I think we have to consider it. He's the one who was connected to the coins." She shook her head. "Nah, it's probably Holmes."

"What about Mrs. Holmes?" suggested Kevin. "You guys met her. What do you think?"

"She's rich," said Nattie. "What would be her motive?"

Kevin rubbed the back of his neck. "I don't know. Her connection to Rance Callahan always struck me the wrong way."

"What connection?" asked Nattie, eyes boring down on her brother.

"In 2008 Ginger Holmes wrote five three-hundred-dollar checks to Rance Callahan."

"Why now?" asked Nattie.

"'Why now,' what?" returned Kevin.

"Why did you wait until now to tell me about Ginger Holmes and Rance Callahan?"

Kevin scrunched the right side of his face as he looked first at Nattie, then Knox, and finally back at Nattie. "Didn't I tell you that? I guess things were progressing so well at her husband, I didn't figure this would matter."

"It may not have mattered then, but it sure matters now," said Nattie.

"When will we be calling on Mrs. Holmes?" asked Knox.

"Tomorrow morning," answered Nattie.

"Good," said Knox. "I didn't like her anyway."

"And we do like Jack," added Kevin.

"I like him, too," confessed Nattie, "but that doesn't mean he's innocent."

"But the timing doesn't make a lot of sense to me," said Knox. "I mean, why now? If he took those coins and buried them on Bays Mountain, then why didn't he dig them up as soon as that investigation ended? That was four years ago. Why now?"

Nattie nodded, "Why now, indeed?"

CHAPTER 45

Out with Alice [Jack]

ONCE A MONTH ALICE AND I WOULD MAKE A TREK over to the Earth Fare in Johnson City. I'm the designated driver. While she shops, which can take anywhere from thirty to sixty minutes, I head over to the deli. On the way I sample everything I can. It's not like Sam's, where you could make a meal out of the samples on a Friday or a Saturday, but it's an appetizer. And it's free.

As she makes her way across the store, I settle into a booth with whatever I'm reading. Today it's a nostalgic read, *God Bless You, Mr. Rosewater,* which was my favorite Kurt Vonnegut novel when I was in college. At least that's how I remember it from forty years ago. I always have a large coffee while I read, and I try to pace myself so that it lasts until Alice shows up with the I'm-ready-for-your-credit-card look. I always get a pastry as well, but with that I need the evidence to be gone before Alice peeks around the corner. This day it was a vegan chocolate chip scone. I'm a big fan of vegan pastry. The vegans restrict their diet in a lot of ways, but they have no problem with sugar.

"Here's what I got for tomorrow," Alice told me when I joined her in the checkout line. She pointed at the section of her cart with a box of fancy crackers, two kinds of cheese, some grapes, a couple of pears, and a couple of apples.

I gave her a thumbs-up without looking close enough to notice what kind of cheeses or crackers she had chosen. I'd be happy with anything she chose—not so much because I am such a good eater, but because she'd make sure it would suit me.

"What's tomorrow?" I asked.

"The Chicago concert," she reminded me.

"Funfest."

A Tomy Thai restaurant is across the street from Earth Fare. We usually get takeout because I don't want to pay so much extra for something to drink, but on this day I thought we had something to celebrate, so we dined in. We both ordered the Phanaeng Curry with extra peanuts. I got mine hot, Alice got hers mild, although I can't tell the difference.

We finished eating at about the same time. She took two-thirds of hers home for a couple of lunches the next week. Mine was gone.

"Rita's," I suggested. Rita's is an Italian ice place that's right on the way home.

"Okay, but let's sit and talk first."

"Okay, what do you want to talk about?"

She tipped her head forward and looked at me over the top of her glasses. "Celebration," she hinted in a high voice.

"'Celebration,'" I repeated. I can't believe I had forgotten why we were eating out. I leaned forward. "Doug called me this morning. The city manager thanked him for helping us out but told him we don't need him anymore."

She didn't look as excited as I thought she would.

"You knew this was coming, didn't you? They all told you it was temporary, right?"

"Talk is cheap," I told her.

She reached out, giving my hand a squeeze. "I'm glad it makes you feel better. I feel bad I didn't know it was still bothering you. I thought it was over when they arrested that lawyer."

"I know. That should have done it, but still, this feels like a weight has been lifted off my back."

"So, what's Doug going to do now?"

That's the kind of question she would have asked. And now that she asked me the question, it sounds like the obvious thing for me to have asked.

She chortled. "You didn't ask him, did you?"

I flashed her my best cute-little-boy grin.

"Men," she sighed.

"Yeah," I agreed. "Men."

A serious look crossed her face. "As long as you were worrying about your job anyway, did you ever think about what you'd do if . . . you know."

"If I got fired?" I finished her sentence. "I figured I'd go work at Lowe's or Home Depot. They like to hire people who know what they're talking about."

She smiled. "I'm glad it didn't come to that, but it's nice to know you were ready just in case."

"I got something else to tell you."

My tone must have been ominous because the serious look returned to her face.

"I've got a nest egg I haven't told you about."

She didn't ask the obvious question. *You see, women do that, too,* I thought, without saying it out loud.

"Yeah. You remember how we were saving up for Sally's wedding?"

She nodded.

"Well, after her wedding I just kept putting that money aside. We were already living without it."

"That's great, honey."

"Thanks, but I have to give credit to Doug. It was his idea."

"I was wondering how we afforded that St. Lucia trip."

"That's how," I told her.

She scrunched up across from me like she was about to giggle. "How much do we have?"

"It's a little hard to say."

Her head twitched to the left as she squinted.

"I've been buying gold coins from the mint. Mostly I've been buying the First Spouse series."

"So what's it worth?"

"I'm guessing, but I'd say between forty-five and fifty thousand dollars."

CHAPTER 46

Ginger Holmes

"THANKS FOR LETTING ME TAG ALONG," said Knox as she turned down the volume. They were driving to Kingsport for an appointment with Ginger Holmes. The radio was on the Adele Pandora station.

"You don't have to thank me, Knox. It's nice having another set of eyes and ears. You see and hear things I miss."

"Thank you for that, too," said Knox softly.

"What?" asked Nattie.

"Encouragement. Most people treat me like I'm some sort of doll, but you never do. You treat me like I have something to offer."

"Well, you do."

They listened to Adele for a while before Nattie asked, "How are things between you and my brother? You seem like you're getting along real well."

"He's great. I mean, I know he's a goofball, but he's real smart, too." Knox gritted her teeth and hunched her shoulders. "I'm sorry. I don't mean anything bad about him."

Nattie laughed. "Please. I know you're on his side. He is a goofball, and if you're going to have a relationship with him, then you need to be able to handle that."

Knox watched Nattie sheepishly.

"For what's it's worth, I think you handle him better than anyone else ever has. Even my mother noticed."

"Really?"

"Yes. She told me she thought you 'brought the Kevin out in him.'"

Knox flushed.

"I think so, too," said Nattie.

"He does that for me, too, you know."

"I can see that," said Nattie. "But he's still a goofball."

"For sure," agreed Knox, "but you watch. One day one of his goofball ideas will pay off."

"I am watching and I'm sure you're right, but when his big idea pays off, he'll still be a goofball."

Knox smiled contentedly. "True, but I like that about him."

"Me, too," admitted Nattie. "But that doesn't keep me from wanting to hold him under water sometimes."

"Me, too," confessed Knox.

They snickered for a moment, then the mood turned serious in the car. Even Adele seemed to grow more somber.

"How about Nathan?" asked Knox.

"Are you asking me if I ever want to hold Nathan under water?"

"No, I'm asking what's going on with you and him."

Nattie glanced over at Knox as she contemplated giving her a blow-off answer. "I think we're done." The words caught in her throat, which surprised her. She breathed a deep, deliberate breath.

"You love him," observed Knox.

Another deep, deliberate breath. "I can't help that, but I can't live with his bull either."

"I thought he was getting help with all that."

"I thought so, too," sighed Nattie, "but he pulled another disappearing act."

"How long has it been since you heard from him?"

"You were there," answered Nattie. "The last I've seen or heard from him was when he walked out of my office."

"That's just been a couple of days, though."

"Maybe so, but if he's manic and he's drinking, it'll be a while. And it will end ugly." Nattie turned her head away from Knox before softly saying, "I want no part of that."

Reaching out, Knox stroked Nattie's shoulder twice. They rode the rest of the way in silence.

* * *

"Thanks for seeing us," said Nattie, stepping through the doorway.

"No problem, really," said Ginger. "I meant it when I said I'd do anything to help you make sure that Presly gets what coming to him." Seeing Knox entering behind Nattie, she added, "And I see you brought your little friend."

"Nice hair," said Nattie.

"Really," fawned Ginger. "I'm glad you like it." Shutting the door behind Knox, she continued, "Please come in." She began leading them across the living room toward the same sunroom where she had entertained them previously.

Halfway across the living room Nattie stopped in front of the fireplace. Pointing at the painting above the mantel she said, "That looks like a Suzanne Barrett Justis painting." The painting was a portrait of a turkey buzzard with the artist's singular attention to the minutest of details.

"It is," said Ginger. "Do you know her? She's local, you know."

"Do you mind if I take a picture?" asked Knox.

"Of course not," answered Ginger.

As Knox took her photograph Nattie explained, "I don't know her myself, but my husband—I mean my ex-husband—and I have eaten at the Mustard Seed Café, and her studio is right next to the restaurant. We've watched her through the window a couple of times."

Ginger smiled and nodded.

"That's not the same picture that was hanging there when we came before, is it?" asked Nattie.

"It isn't?" responded Ginger, sounding surprised. "Maybe not. We change that piece out pretty often."

Sure you do, thought Nattie.

When Knox put her phone away, Ginger said, "I don't want to be rude, but can we please move this along? I have a meeting to get to as soon as we are finished."

"Lead the way," said Nattie.

Once they were all seated in the sunroom, Ginger said, "I know you arrested Presly about a month ago, so I assume you're here to get information for his trial. Is that correct?"

As far as you know, thought Nattie before lying. "Yes, it is. We want to ask you about Presly's partner, a Mr. Rance Callahan. What can you tell us about him?"

Ginger's face screwed up, then—looking directly at Nattie without blinking—she said, "I don't recognize that name."

"Really," said Nattie, matching Ginger's stare.

"Does that surprise you?" asked Ginger indignantly.

"A little," said Nattie. "So you don't know how he and your husband got together?"

"My ex-husband," corrected Ginger.

"Do you know how Mr. Callahan and your ex-husband got together?"

"How would I?"

"Well, Mr. Callahan was a private investigator who took money from wives, like you, and then blackmailed their husbands with the information he was hired by the wives to gather." She paused, studying Ginger, who was working hard to maintain her stoic posture. "Does that sound familiar to you?"

Ginger stood suddenly. "Not in the least." Her head shook a little as she shuddered. "Now, if you'll excuse me, my high school graduating class is having a minireunion at the Chicago concert on Sunday, and I'm on the organizing committee."

Nattie took her time rising to her feet. "Thank you for your time."

"I hope your reunion is a success," said Knox as she stood. "That should be a great concert."

* * *

As they drove down the winding drive Knox asked, "Did you get what you were looking for?"

"I wasn't sure what I was looking for when we drove over here, but now I know."

"Did you find it?"

"Actually," smiled Nattie, "I'm hoping you'll find it."

"Me?"

"Do you remember the painting that was over her fireplace when we came the first time?"

"The one she told me I couldn't photograph?"

"Yes, that one. You got a picture of it anyway, didn't you?"

Knox smiled.

"Do you still have it?"

"I sure do," declared Knox. "I'll forward it to you. Do you think it has something to do with the theft?"

"I don't know," said Nattie. "I came here with questions about Rance Callahan and Presly Holmes. Now I have questions about Ginger Holmes, too. The biggest question is about that painting."

CHAPTER 47

The Chicago Concert

"LOOK WHO'S HERE," SAID KEVIN EXCITEDLY as he began weaving his way across the football field. Neither Knox nor Nattie saw whatever he had seen, but they followed him through the crowd.

When they caught up to him, Kevin was unfolding his camp chair. Not until they were right next to him did Nattie realize that they were joining Jack and Alice Stout, who were in camp chairs of their own. Next to Alice was Doug Hout.

Jack immediately stood as Nattie and Knox arrived. He offered to take the camp chair each had strapped over their shoulder.

"I wondered if we'd see you here," said Alice as Jack got their chairs set up.

Jack arranged the chairs in an oval, which meant the three newcomers were seated with their backs to the stage. "You can swing these around when the music starts," he assured them.

"Thank you," said Nattie and Knox simultaneously.

"This is my wife, Alice," Jack said, looking at Knox.

Knox stepped toward Alice and extended her hand. "I'm Knox."

"And this is our friend Doug," said Alice after shaking Knox's hand. "He works with Jack."

Doug remained seated but acknowledged the introduction with a wave of his hand.

"Would you like something to eat?" asked Alice. In front of her was a small camp table supporting a Tupperware box of cheese slices, a box of crackers, and a bag of fruit.

"We've got Zero's," announced Kevin. He had volunteered to bring refreshments. He opened the backpack he had worn in and took out a sub sandwich and passed it to Nattie. "Veggie deluxe for you."

He handed a second sub to Knox. "A veggie deluxe with hot pepper relish for you."

"Italian sausage for you," guessed Knox.

He nodded yes as he began unwrapping his sandwich.

"So you and Jack work together," said Nattie.

"We used to," said Doug. "I'm going back into retirement, where I belong."

"That's right," blurted Alice. "Jack told me that. Are you going back to Arizona?"

"Nope," Doug declared. "I believe my niece would hunt me down if I did that. She's bugged me ever since I lost Franny to come back here, and once I got here she's done everything she can to set me up permanent."

"That's the truth," came a female voice from behind Nattie.

The comment, coming from so close behind her, gave Nattie a start. She turned to discover that the speaker was Kayleigh Buckner, Doug Hout's niece.

"He's going to stay with us, and tomorrow he's going to begin working on the Carousel project," continued Kayleigh.

"You're the wolf lady," said Kevin, pointing at Kayleigh.

"That's right," agreed Knox.

Kayleigh, for the first time, took notice of the people she was speaking over. "Oh, hi," she said, looking down at Knox and Kevin. Noticing Nattie, who sat directly below her, last, she nodded and smiled.

Nattie nodded back.

"Would you like to join us, Kayleigh?" asked Alice. "We've got plenty of snacks."

"I would love to," said Kayleigh, "but I'm meeting my graduating class here. We're having a minireunion because a lot of my class is back for the Chicago concert."

"Have a good time," said Doug dismissively.

"Thanks, Uncle Doug," said Kayleigh warmly. "The reason I came over was to ask if you could give me a ride tomorrow afternoon."

"Sure thing. What time?" asked Doug.

"Can I call you about that? I'll be at a Class of '97 luncheon. I'm not sure when it'll end."

"No problem. Where?"

"It's at the Holmeses' house on the hill. Do you know where that is?"

"Yep."

"Thanks," said Kayleigh. Lifting her hand in a wave, she scanned the group, "Good to see you all. Enjoy the concert."

As soon as Kayleigh turned to leave, Jack stood and said, "I'll be right back."

"Hurry," Alice told him. "It looks like they're getting ready on stage."

Jack nodded but showed no sign of hurrying as he left.

As they began doing sound checks from the stage, Kevin stood up and said, "I guess it's time to rearrange ourselves."

Once they were settled into their new seating arrangements, with Nattie directly in front of Doug, she overheard Alice say, "Thanks for getting Jack started collecting gold coins."

"No big deal," Doug told her. "Us Houts have been into coin collecting forever."

CHAPTER 48

Sunday

NATTIE BARELY SLEPT ON SATURDAY NIGHT. The question about the coins plagued her until she was finally too exhausted to stay awake any longer. Then she woke up to the same nagging questions: Why were the coins missing from Holmes's list? Why were they not stored with the other items? Who took them? Who hid them on Bays Mountain? Why there? Why now?

What was it Alice said last night? pondered Nattie. *She thanked Doug Hout for getting Jack interested in coins.*

Could Jack, or maybe Jack and Doug, have stolen those coins after all?

She shook her head gently in an effort to clear her mind. She sat up in bed for the same reason.

The timing is off for Doug, she reminded herself. *The Bays Mountain coins were already found while he was still in Arizona.*

She decided she needed a change of scene, so she got dressed and headed downtown to Manna Bagel. She hoped she wouldn't see anyone, but thought that early Sunday morning would be okay.

After ordering, Nattie settled into her favorite spot adjacent to the front door in the alcove.

Her mind drifted off again. *Why did Doug come back to Kingsport now? Had he heard the coins were found? Was he involved with Jack, but afraid Jack was cheating him?*

She shook her head no. *Those two men don't look like they're the least bit suspicious of each other. Besides, if it is Jack, we still need to explain why the coins aren't on Holmes's list.*

Nattie didn't notice when her breakfast sandwich arrived.

Her sausage and egg bagel sat untouched on the table as she sipped her coffee and stared out the front window.

She was so lost in thought that she didn't notice Nathan walk up to the window and stare back at her. When she finally noticed him standing there, grinning at her, her eye roll was involuntary.

Nathan circled around through the door and sat across from her. Ignoring the blank stare he was receiving, he placed an envelope on the table. "Are you going to eat that?" he asked.

"Have you been drinking?" she snapped.

Startled, he sat back. "Well, you don't waste any time, do you?"

"I don't have much time," she said, "so why don't you start by answering my question?"

"Not a drop," he bragged. "I've been working, and you're going to want to see what I found out."

"You've been working, have you? What have you been doing that kept you so busy that you couldn't even call me to say what you were doing?"

"So, you don't hear from me for a couple of days, and you automatically assume I'm on a bender," he said indignantly.

"'A couple of days,'" she repeated loud enough to turn the heads of a group of college girls at the big table in the center of the room. "It was Wednesday when you walked out. That's not just a couple of days."

"Okay. You're right. I should have called," he conceded. "But honestly, I haven't been drinking."

"What then?"

His eyes lit up, and he beamed. "I was pretty mad when I left. I drove through the night so that I could be at the Federation Fidelity office first thing Thursday morning. I was sure they were cheating us."

"You were sure," stated Nattie. "Not now?"

"Calm down," he told her with a shake of his finger. It was a gesture that infuriated her. "Be patient. I'll tell you everything you want to know. Just let me tell it my way."

She looked at her watch. "You got ten minutes."

"Same old Nattie," he grinned. If he thought he could charm her by teasing, the thought evaporated under her steely expression. In a more serious tone he began, "I spent half the day being shuffled from one suit to another in Indianapolis, and then they sent me up to Chicago. That's why I was there first thing Friday morning."

"So you didn't sleep for a second night," observed Nattie. "Your counselor told you to watch that."

"She said with bipolar I won't always need sleep, but to make sure to get rest in darkness anyway."

"I know. I was there."

"Well, it worked out that I didn't need much sleep, didn't it? Besides, I caught a few hours in the car Friday morning outside of the Federation office in Chicago."

"What'd you find out on Friday?"

He slid the envelope closer to her. "It's all in there. I meant to get it to you Saturday afternoon, but I went to sleep when I got home early Saturday morning and I didn't wake up until this morning."

As she picked up the envelope she slid her breakfast bagel across to him.

The first pages she held up were a copy of the document detailing what art items had been recovered and their value. "This is the same as the one we got before."

He nodded yes as he chewed.

The other document she found in the envelope was a copy of the original appraisal of the insured items. She studied it intently for as long as it took him to finish her breakfast.

As he was finishing the last bite, he mumbled, "I told you you'd want to see that."

Her face was buried in her cell phone as she scrolled for something. When she found what she was looking for, she lit up. "I'll say," she agreed. She looked right at Nathan. "This is good."

"Did you figure something out?"

"I figured this out," she said with a tip of her head. "Federation didn't cheat us."

"I got that figured," he said.

She tapped her finger on the pages as they lay on the table in front of her. "I think this does clear a couple of things up. I need to go back to the office and compare this list to Presly's list first. And I need you to do something, too."

"Anything," he said eagerly.

"Do you have a good contact in the Kingsport PD?"

"Todd Hare," confirmed Nathan.

"Do you remember telling me that there was a witness who saw Jack Stout on Bays Mountain the day before those gold coins were found there?"

He nodded again.

"I want to know who that witness was. Can your friend Todd help us out?"

CHAPTER 49

The Luncheon

[Four hours later]

"WHAT ARE WE WAITING FOR?" ASKED NATHAN. They were sitting in Nattie's car outside of Ginger Holmes's house.

"That," said Nattie, pointing at the entry where two women were saying good-bye to Ginger Holmes. "I was waiting for the last of the guests to leave."

They watched as the two women stepped into the only other car in the driveway and drove off. As soon as they were out of sight, Nattie, followed closely by Nathan, marched to the front door and knocked.

Ginger Holmes answered the door sporting a huge smile. The smile disappeared as soon as she made eye contact with Nattie. "I don't know what you want, but whatever it is, now isn't a good time. I just hosted a luncheon."

"Kayleigh, Kayleigh Buckner," said Nattie, pointing past Ginger to where Kayleigh was standing between the foyer and the living room.

As Ginger turned around to see what Nattie was pointing at, Nattie slipped past her into the foyer. "Hey," objected Ginger, stepping toward Nattie. The move allowed Nathan the opportunity to enter as well.

"You," Ginger growled at Nattie, "you can take your sidekick and get out of my house."

Nattie just smiled and pointed at the couch. "I think we should all sit."

"This is breaking and entering. I'll have you arrested," threatened Ginger.

"Technically you opened the door to us, so we didn't break in at all," said Nattie as she made herself comfortable on the leather sofa facing the fireplace. "You did ask us to leave, and since we aren't going to do as you ask, you have every right to call the police and have us removed."

"Kayleigh," called Ginger, "call 911." She was still standing in the entry, arms folded and tapping her right foot nervously.

Kayleigh didn't move as she was paying more attention to Nattie than Ginger. Her shirt sleeves were rolled up. She had a dish towel in her hands.

"Yes, Kayleigh, call 911," said Nattie, "and then come on in and help Ginger explain that." She pointed at the painting hanging over the mantle.

Nathan, who was also still standing in the entry, stepped alongside of Ginger and extended his right hand, palm up, toward the living room. "Shall we?"

Ginger stopped tapping her foot and scowled at him.

"That's okay, Nathan. She's already seen this, but you should come over here and take a look. Have you ever seen a three-and-a-half-million-dollar painting?"

"I saw the *Mona Lisa* once," he said as he walked around behind the couch where Nattie remained seated. "That is not the *Mona Lisa.* He looks familiar. Who is that?"

"That's Bob Barker."

"That is Bob Barker," said Ginger. "I own that painting. I can prove it."

"You have a receipt, do you?" asked Nathan.

"I certainly do."

"Is it dated?" he asked.

"Of course."

"And I'll bet you've had it over five years, haven't you?"

Her head shook as she said, "Try ten."

"I'm confused," said Nathan in a sarcastically innocent voice. "Is that before or after the robbery?"

"Before," answered Nattie quickly.

"Is that a problem?" asked Nathan in the same voice.

"Not for me," smirked Nattie. "But four years ago Federation Fidelity paid three and a half million for it." To Ginger she added, "Their right of ownership is more recent than yours. But you knew that, didn't you? That's why you put it away when you knew I was coming that first time."

Ginger just stared.

"Still want to call the police?" asked Nattie.

All Ginger would say was, "Bitch."

Nattie laughed. "I thought you might say that, but don't worry about calling the police. I took care of that for you. They should be here any minute now."

"You think you're so smart," snapped Ginger.

"That's because she is," bragged Nathan. "She figured you out."

"You know nothing," spewed Ginger.

"I know that you lied about knowing Rance Callahan. I know that you hired him knowing that he'd tell Presly you were planning to divorce him. I know you knew he'd set up the insurance coverage in just his name, and then he'd rob it himself. And knowing all that allowed you to take out the one art piece you wanted to protect."

Ginger forced a single "Ha. You can't prove any of that."

"I'm afraid I can," said Nattie. She then turned to Kayleigh, who was still standing meekly at the edge of the living room, fidgeting with her eyebrow. "You got the coins, didn't you?"

Kayleigh, looking as lost as Ginger looked outraged, came all the way into the living room and flopped down in a chair adjacent to the sofa.

"She couldn't have done any of it without you, could she? You knew exactly which contractor would botch the construction because your uncle, the building inspector, told you. And you knew exactly what Rance Callahan would do when Ginger hired him because you knew that Presly got him out of several jams before that."

Kayleigh just stared at her, a tear welling up in the corner of her eye.

"The evidence is in the documents," began Nattie, "and you're the only one who was in a position to alter them. I'm sure it was easy to get Presly to sign the original policy without looking too closely at it. And it was even easier to create a version that didn't include the Bob Barker painting or the coin collection."

Nattie had been maintaining eye contact with Kayleigh, but she paused to glance at Ginger, who still stood glaring at her. "You had to keep those things in because they had to watch the original appraisal, right, Ginger?"

Ginger didn't answer.

Turning back to Kayleigh, Nattie asked, "Presly never knew he had been set up, did he?"

"Don't say anything, Kayleigh," threatened Ginger.

Ignoring Ginger, Nattie repeated the question, "He didn't, did he, Kayleigh?"

Looking down, Kayleigh shook her head no.

"You fool," barked Ginger.

"It's over, Ginger. They know," sighed Kayleigh. She looked at Nattie woefully. "How did you know?"

"It was the coins. It was so curious that those coins showed up on Bays Mountain four years after they were stolen. I kept asking myself, *Why now?* until I realized you were the only one who benefited from the timing."

Ginger disappeared out the front door.

Nathan started after her, but Nattie called out, "Let her be. She's got nowhere to go."

He returned to his spot behind the couch.

"You had the coins all along. Probably selling them a few at a time. Those are fairly untraceable. But then your aunt died, and the timing was right to get your uncle to move back. All you had to do was get him his old job back."

Kayleigh began to cry.

"You were the one who planted those coins on Bays Mountain, and then you were the one who claimed to have seen Jack Stout there just before they were found."

She stuttered, "I just wanted to get my uncle back. That's all I wanted. Is that so bad?"

"That's not bad," declared Nattie. "But did you think about what would happen to Jack Stout in all of this?"

Kayleigh stared back at her without answering.

"You weren't just going to cost him his job. You could have landed him in prison."

Two uniformed policemen entered through the still-open front door. Todd Hare, Nathan's contact in the Kingsport Police Department, was the first one to enter. "Kayleigh Buckner?" he asked.

"I'm Kayleigh," she said, standing up.

"You're under arrest," he told her before reading her her rights.

Kayleigh was docile, almost catatonic, as she was handcuffed and led from the room. At the door she turned and looked pitifully toward Nattie. "When did you suspect me?"

"When I first met you at the lawyer's office I noticed you had an incredible memory for dates. And behind your desk was a shrine to the wolves on Bays Mountain. I knew you were lying when you said you didn't remember the date of the robbery. It was December 4, 2009, the night the wolves escaped Bays Mountain."

Names in *Why Now?*

** a real person whose name is used with creative license
 * a real person as they really are

A. Morris** artist

A. Cullop** artist

Alice Stout Jack's wife

Ava* waitress at Betty's Stockyard Café

Avery Heart owner of Heart Construction

Barbara* owner of Pretty Girls Station

Beau Robinette former Cop; Counselor; Chef; Nattie's friend

Brittney* Manna Bagel

C. Tidman** artist

Carl and Sue Matherly** owners of Nutty Java II

Carlton DeMarco Kingsport City attorney

Carol* waitress at Perkins

Charlotte Stevens Nathan's Counselor

Cynthia Horton Hale** member of F.B.I. squad

D. Buck** artist

Daniel kid being bullied on bus; Jack's friend

Doug Lightfeather Hout former Kingsport building inspector

Dyan** receptionist for Charlotte Stevens

E. Rhymer** artist

Elijah Gorzilanski Nattie's nephew

Franny Hout Doug's wife

Ginger Holmes Presly's ex-wife

Gregory Peppa Nathan's psychiatrist

Hiram Moreland retired P.I.; Nattie's mentor

Ingrid O'Brien Nattie's Mother

J. Hensley** artist

Janice Chafin* owner of The Enchanted Florist

Jack Stout Kingsport building inspector

Joe Tennis* author of Haunts of Virginia's Blue Ridge Highlands

John and Karen Vann* friends of the O'Brien's

Juniper (Juney) Jack's youngest daughter

Karen Rohr** F.B.I. Agent in Chattanooga

Kayleigh Buckner** receptionist for lawyer Presly Holmes

Kenneth* Ruritan club member

Kevin Johnson Nattie's brother & office manager

Knox DeVilla (Candace Farmer) singer; dating Kevin

Lionel O'Brien Nattie's stepfather

Mary Jane* Kenneth's wife

Mark Buckner Kayleigh's husband

Matt Richardson* Young Life staff

Micah Jack's grandson

Miranda Nattie's deceased friend

Moe Ross** FBI agent

Natalie Moreland Nattie

Nathan Johnson Nattie's dad

Nathan Moreland Nattie's ex-husband

Patty* Manager of Pretty Girl Station

Presly Holmes Kingsport lawyer; his art collection was stolen

Rance Callahan owner of The Saloon in Chattanooga

Sally Jack and Alice's oldest daughter

Sam Jack's grandson; Sally's son

Samantha Gorzilanski Nattie's stepsister

Shannon Heart Avery Heart's wife

Sunny Hill Nattie sent her to prison in Why Bristol?

Suzanne Barrett Justis* Kingsport artist

Suzy Lawson* Ruritan member

The Wolf Nattie and Kevin's grandfather

Todd Hare** Kingsport Police Department

Trace Noble Nattie sent him to prison in Why Me?

Tessa Jack's middle daughter; Micah's mother

Trevor Samantha's son

For other titles, authors blog, photos,
and discount codes:

www.csthompsonbooks.com

Other titles in the WHY MYSTERY series:

Why Natasha?

Why Him?

Why Me?

Why Bristol?

Why Knox?